FINDERS KEEPERS

N.R. WALKER

COPYRIGHT

Cover Artist: Humble Nations
Editor: Labyrinth Bound Edits
Finders Keepers © 2018 N.R. Walker
Publisher: BlueHeart Press

All Rights Reserved:

Trademarks:

Warning

Intended for an 18+ audience only. This book contains material that maybe offensive to some and is intended for a mature, adult audience. It contains graphic language, explicit sexual content, and adult situations.

N.R. WALKER

Finders Keepers

BLURB

Needing a change of scene, Griffin Burke moves from Brisbane to Coolum Beach to start a new job. The beautiful white sand, aqua-coloured ocean, blue skies, and summer breezes are everything he longs for. What he finds is a mud-covered dog, lost and hungry, with a nametag and a phone number.

Dane Hughes is stuck in Surfers Paradise at a week-long work conference when he gets a phone call from his distraught mother. His dog, his fur baby, Wicket, has run away. Unable to leave and feeling helpless and miserable, he gets a text from a guy. "I think I found your dog..."

Griffin and Dane start talking, and Griffin agrees to look after Wicket until Dane can collect him. With a few days left before his new job starts, Griffin takes Wicket on some coastal adventures and sends Dane photos of their fun, and so the start of something new and kind of wonderful begins.

Griffin might have moved to Coolum in search of a new life, but what he finds is so much more. What he gets to keep just might take some four-legged help.

CHAPTER ONE

GRIFFIN BURKE

MOVING from Brisbane to Coolum Beach wasn't exactly a hardship. I mean, Coolum was on the Sunshine Coast, which meant tropical beaches, warm breezes, and hot surfer dudes to ogle. And that was while I was at work.

I hoped my days off would be much the same.

I'd broken up with my boyfriend Nick, six months ago. It was an amicable split; we'd been best friends forever and took the plunge into boyfriend territory, and somewhere in our two years together, our spark had petered out to nothing more than a warm friendly glow. And he was still my friend, but there was a void now where our relationship had once been.

I had an itch I couldn't quite reach.

But it wasn't just Nick. It was everything. At twenty-four, our circle of friends was all focusing on careers, and our social lives had dwindled to a once or twice a month get together. We were all overworked and underpaid, too broke or tired to go out for drinks, all while trying to save every cent we made with little to no hope of breaking into the property market.

There were jokes about Millennials and avocado toast, but I'm telling you. That shit is real.

My job working at the front desk at the Stamford Plaza in Brisbane paid well, don't get me wrong. But in the city, it wasn't enough to get ahead on. I loved my job, and under the wing and watchful eye of Ludo, it had been a crash course in excellence and the highest of standards. He was a middle-aged Belgian man with a Dali-esque moustache and eagle eyes who, for reasons I couldn't explain, had taken a liking to me. Maybe it was because I was the utmost professional; maybe he saw something in me. Maybe it was because we were the only two gay men on the front desk. Whatever the reason, I was grateful.

He'd taught me well. So well, in fact, that I leapfrogged my co-workers to land in management. Ludo had said my demeanour and etiquette reminded him of those films of the Victorian era, and I, like some courtier, treated all hotel guests as if they were royalty. Not in a smarmy way as others did, but in a genuine way. And it was that honest integrity, he'd said, that would take me far.

And he was right. It took me two hours north, to Coolum Beach Emporium, a five-star resort on the Sunshine Coast. My new job was the next step up for me, and it was Ludo's professional recommendation that sealed my application. The truth was, if he didn't get rid of me, I was, in all likelihood, next in line for his job. So, when I'd applied for a promotion elsewhere, he did what any self-serving, job-preserving person would do. He recommended me for the job, not for my benefit, but for his own. I didn't blame him one bit.

Because I soon figured out where that itch was.

I had itchy feet.

And I'm not talking about some gross fungal foot infection. It was a metaphorical itch that only a sea-change could scratch.

I wanted more. I wanted a new life. I needed a change. I needed to move on, start over somewhere where the sun wasn't blocked by skyscrapers and traffic congestion. My days of clubbing and one-night stands were well behind me. I wasn't interested in that anymore. I wanted coffee in slow and friendly cafés, hikes in the mountains, sunsets over the beach.

So when the position of front desk, second-level management at Coolum came up, I grabbed it with both hands.

I packed up my tiny flat into a removalist truck, loaded up my car, and headed north. I'd found a one-bedroom place in Coolum, above some old lady's house. Apparently, it had once been one big house, built with a self-contained apartment on the second floor for the owner's parents. It had an open living area, small kitchen and bathroom, and my own laundry. There was even a balcony that overlooked the hinterland. At some point it had been closed off to the rest of the house, probably when the new owners realised the upstairs could be leased out to help supplement their home loan. But there was a yard, a lock-up garage, the greenest trees I'd ever seen hiding all the neighbours from view, and it sure as hell beat living in an apartment complex.

Rent was cheap enough, given the terms of my lease agreement: for a reduced weekly rent, all I had to do was help the old lady downstairs out by mowing her lawn once a week. How hard could it be? I mean, I'd mown my parents' lawn every week since I was a kid. The lawnmower was provided. I'd seen the yard on my rental inspection when I'd signed the lease. It'd take me thirty minutes, tops.

Easy peasy.

So I got all moved into my new place and had everything unpacked on day one. I'd met my downstairs landlady for the first time as the two bulky removalists were lugging my bed up the stairs. I was at the bottom of the stairs watching them, not entirely ogling, when a tiny, five-foot-tall woman stood beside me.

She didn't say anything for a while, just stared at the men straining to get the wooden bedhead up the flight of stairs. Still without looking at me, she hummed. "Nice arse."

I almost choked on my sip of water. "Uh..."

"Don't tell me you weren't looking. I might be a little hard of hearing, but I ain't blind."

Right then.

I held out my hand. "Name's Griffin Burke."

She shook my hand, and her hard, firm grip surprised me. She looked kind of frail at first, but then I noticed her tattoos. Her entire right arm was now a mottled, wrinkled mass of blue and coloured ink on sun-leathered skin. Given she looked to be in her seventies, she must have had a full sleeve done forty or fifty years ago.

Jesus.

"Bernice Warren."

She was wearing a sleeveless tank top and a flowing skirt. Upon closer inspection, she looked like a hippy that peace, love, and time forgot. Her face had seen too much sun as well, wrinkled and leathered, though I imagined she would have once been stunningly beautiful. Her blue eyes still had spark, her long hair, once blonde, was now ash grey.

"Come with me," she said, turning on her heel and walking toward the roller door. When she turned, I noticed her left arm. Old, mottled blue tattoos went to her elbow, as well as two scars that looked like lightning strikes. They looked surgical and my first thought was shoulder reconstruction, but then I noticed one scar ran underneath her shirt and up her neck. She turned the latch on the roller door, and using her right arm only, lifted the door to review a storage space. Inside was a lawnmower, wheelbarrow, and some gardening tools.

Ah, right. I was the resident mower of lawns.

"I'd do it myself," she said. "But the old arm doesn't work like it used to." She lifted her left arm rigidly. It didn't hang useless but there was definitely restricted movement.

"It's fine," I said. "I don't mind mowing lawns at all. My weekends will be Monday and Tuesday though, not Saturday and Sunday. If that's okay?"

"It's fine. Don't much care what day you do 'em." She nodded to herself. "Last tenant was a nice girl. Started out with good intentions, and she was gonna do all sorts of things to help me out, but that didn't last long." Bernice looked up at me and stared for a good long minute. "You're not the churchgoing type, are you?"

"Uh…"

"I don't mind if you are, I just don't wanna offer you one of my special brownies and for you to totally hash out on me and start mumbling biblical shit at me every time you see me."

I fought a smile and lost, and I tried not to laugh but couldn't help that either. "Not biblical. Not in that sense, anyway. Unless you consider my earlier staring at that guy's arse a religion. As for the special brownies, I haven't had any for a while. Not since college, anyway."

Bernice grinned and nodded slowly. "So you know what I mean when I say special brownie. Not like the last poor girl who thought it was my grandma's special recipe or some shit." She shook her head slowly. "Dunno what she was thinking. Do I look like Betty Fucking Crocker to you?"

I barked out a laugh and was now pretty sure I knew why the real estate receptionist had given me an apologetic squint when she handed me the keys and offered a weak, "Good luck."

"No, you don't. But I think you and I are gonna get along just fine."

"Good, good." Bernice closed the roller door and gave me the low down on rubbish collection days, which neighbour was nice, and which was an arsehole. She didn't have any issues with music, as long as I didn't mind it either. She didn't give a shit—her words, not mine—about pets, as long as I cleaned up after them, and as long as I didn't cook meth or with too much garlic, we'd get along just fine.

I liked her immediately.

I told her how I'd moved from Brisbane and had a week before I started my new job. I explained I wanted to get to know the area first and find the best spots along the beach for swimming and hiking, and she gave me the 'I've been here for forty years' rundown. She told me where the locals swam, where they avoided. She told me which supermarket was the best, which café had the best coffee and the cutest baristas, and which bars to avoid during peak tourist season.

So much for it taking me a week to find all that out for myself. I just got the true-local scoop in five minutes.

I still spent the next few days checking it all out though. I wanted to familiarise myself with everything. Not just for me, but for any guests at the hotel who asked tourist-visitor questions. I found myself at the tourist information centre, asking a dozen questions and taking two dozen brochures. I drove all over the Sunshine Coast, visiting each town, walking the streets, and getting a feel for coastal living.

The standard dress code of Coolum seemed to be board shorts, singlet tops, and thongs. It was a coastal town in permanent holiday mode. Kids rode pushbikes or skateboards holding surfboards, their skin sun-kissed and their hair bleached from too much time outside. Even the professionals, like real-estate agents and business owners, seemed to do things on holiday time. The summers were more humid than in Brisbane but the coastal breeze made it bearable. Palm trees and ferns grew out of every available space, and for the first time in a long time, I felt like I could breathe.

This was exactly what I needed.

Three days before I was to start my new job, I drove to the Coolum National Park and pulled into a spot. I grabbed my cap and backpack, double checked I had two bottles of water and gave myself a quick re-spray of insect repellent, locked my car, and set off on the walking trail.

There was nothing quite like hiking in a rainforest. The sounds alone were amazing: cicadas and birds competing in some kind of symphony. And the smell of salt and damp earth was invigorating.

According to the brochures and the internet, the hike starts out pretty easy but as the walk starts to climb Mount Coolum, it gets pretty intense. And they weren't wrong. The track was uneven and steep, the exertion burning in my legs and lungs. I passed people coming back down as I went up, all smiling or with a 'hi' or 'g'day,' and after a kilometre or so, I reached the summit.

The view was spectacular.

I had a three-sixty view of the coast and the hinterland for miles. I took a bunch of photos and selfies, then sent them to my parents and my friends back in Brissy, and I even sent one to my sister. And before my sweat-soaked shirt could dry in the sweltering sun, I headed back down. I made it to the car park, panting and grinning to myself, and sat my arse down on the wooden picnic table in the shade, not far from my car, to catch my breath and let my legs recover.

A small brownish dog came over to me and sat in front of me. He was cute and had a happy face. His pink tongue lolled out of his mouth, and he just sat there and stared. I looked around the car park, but no one seemed to be paying attention.

"Hey there," I said to him.

I'm sure he smiled.

"Where're your parents?" I asked, then realised I was talking to a dog like he was some lost kid.

He just sat there, smiling, tongue lolling.

I took a long drink of my last water bottle, and the dog edged a little closer and licked his lips. "You thirsty?" I asked.

I looked around the car park again and figured no one would be mad if I gave their dog a drink of water. So I cupped one hand in front of his face and poured what was left of my water into it, and the dog lapped at it eagerly until the bottle was drained.

Poor little guy was thirsty.

I looked around again, this time concerned. I mean, it was hot. It was summer. He shouldn't have been left without water. Maybe someone wouldn't be mad at me for giving their dog water, but I could be pissed at his owner for neglecting to do the same.

But there was no one there.

"Where's your mum or dad?" I asked him again, giving his forehead a pat.

He just smiled at me.

"You're a cute little thing, aren't you."

His smile widened.

I wanted to go hit the beach to let my muscles soak in saltwater for a bit, so I collected my bag and walked to my car. The dog followed. Again, I looked around to see if anyone was watching. I couldn't see any people, but there were cars and maybe his owners were hiking. Maybe they'd be back any minute.

Convincing myself that was the case, I said goodbye to my new four-legged friend and got in my car. I cranked up the air conditioning and reversed out, and when I looked up, I saw he'd sat down, watching me with a sad face as I drove away.

I frowned all the way to the beach. But as soon as those aqua-coloured waves came into view, I forgot about the dog and walked into the ocean. I swam for a bit and the cool water soothed my body and cleared my mind. There sure was something medicinal about saltwater.

I dried off and went home, starving hungry, and didn't give that dog one more thought until the next day when I was hoping to do the hike again. It had rained during the night and the path to the top of Mount Coolum was closed. *Impassable from wet-weather* the sign said, and I remembered reading online that after rain, the trail was closed. I sat in my car wondering if I should find another hiking trail or just go straight to the beach when I saw him.

The little brownish dog was now a whole lot more brown, straggly and wet. He sat near the picnic table where I'd given him a drink of water the day before, just watching me.

I opened the door and got out. Not really knowing what I was going to do with him, but I sure as hell wasn't leaving him here. He'd clearly spent the night in the rain, alone, with no food, and most likely scared as hell. I thought he was going to bolt, so I crouched down near my open car door and patted my knee. "Here, boy," I said, trying not to sound or look threatening.

He took off all right, but not away from me. He ran straight toward me, darted around my legs, and jumped into my car.

"Hey," I said, standing up. He wasn't sitting on my driver's seat. He'd perched himself in the passenger seat, just sitting up like he'd been waiting for me to give him a lift. "You right there?"

His pink tongue lolled out of his dirty face. He obviously wasn't dangerous, and he sure didn't look like he was going anywhere. I sat in my seat and closed the door and looked at my new passenger.

"You look like an Ewok."

I'm certain he smiled.

And then I noticed his collar had a name tag. I reached out slowly, gauging his response, but he licked my finger so I assumed we were good. I lifted his name tag and had to rub the mud away so I could read it.

Wicket.

His name was Wicket.

It took me a second, but I got it. Wicket was indeed an Ewok from *Star Wars*. The cute little curious one that meets Princess Leia. "Well, Wicket, I bet someone misses you."

He grinned at me some more.

I turned the name tag over and found a mobile phone number. *Thank God.* I took out my phone and dialled.

CHAPTER TWO

DANE HUGHES

NORMALLY I'D BE STOKED with a week in Surfers Paradise, especially when it was an all-expenses-paid work stint. Sure, the days were kind of boring with hours of meetings, think-tanks, role-plays, and any other initiative-based classes that Australia's largest telco company thought its staff should endure. But the nights were usually dinner and drinks and it was good to hang out on a personal level with other store managers from across Queensland. I only saw these people a few times a year and I loved catching up with them.

And this trip started out just fine, but after a phone call from my distressed mother, all I wanted to do was go home.

I had left my dog with my parents while I was away, and two days ago, I got a phone call from my mum in tears.

Wicket was missing.

"I only left the door unlocked for a second while I went to the mailbox," she cried.

I'd told her a thousand times—she knew from being at my place—that Wicket could jump up, swipe the handle of any screen door, and wait for it to swing open, then be gone like the wind.

And gone, he was.

Mum and Dad lived in Caloundra, twenty kilometres from where I lived in Maroochydore. I'd dropped Wicket off at their place on my way to the Gold Coast, with his food and bed and leash and favourite toys. Dad just had his knee operated on so he couldn't drive, and Mum didn't have a licence. But Mum had called every vet in town and the council pound every few hours. She'd walked the entire suburb, calling his name. Caloundra wasn't exactly a huge city, but it was big enough, and Wicket wasn't familiar with it at all. And to a small dog, it may as well have been an endless maze of one distracting smell after another.

I couldn't leave the course. It was compulsory training, and nothing short of a family emergency was a plausible enough reason to leave. Believe me, I asked.

Taking phone calls mid-course wasn't acceptable either. Guest speakers didn't exactly feel appreciated when mobile phones rang, interrupting their well-rehearsed spiels. It was respectful to switch phones to silent. I could appreciate that.

But I needed updates. And when my phone vibrated in my pocket, I was dying to check it. There was just no way I could. Then, over the next hour, it buzzed again and again. When we were excused for lunch, I already had my phone out and was walking toward the door before anyone had even stood up. I had two missed calls, two voicemails, and four texts, all from an unknown number. And one text from my mother. I read hers first.

Still no luck

I frowned, and with a heavy sigh, I read the other text messages. One was from Li, my right-hand woman at work.

I'd left her in charge and had no doubt in her ability to run a smooth shop. Her message was just to let me know all was well but if I could give her a quick call when I could. The next message was from my brother.

Mum told me about Wicket. Dad's pissed he can't drive the streets looking for him too. Let me know what you need me to do.

A pang of hopelessness squeezed my heart. I was touched that my younger brother wanted to help, but he was at uni in Brisbane. What could he possibly do from there? And I loved that my whole family was so concerned, but I was heartsick that I was hundreds of kilometres away doing nothing while Wicket was lost.

I tried not to think about what he was going through. If he was hurt, hungry, scared. Had he been hit by a car? I'd heard horror stories of dogs being stolen for dog-fighting. Oh God, Wicket wouldn't stand a chance...

Please, dear God, no.

I checked the last text.

Hi. I left some voicemails... I think I found your dog.

I blinked and reread the text.

They left a message. I fumbled for the voicemail and paced until the recording started to play. Then I stopped in my tracks.

Um, hi. Hello. My name is Griffin. Um, could you please return my call? Thanks.

The message ended abruptly, which was strange. It was a guy's voice and he never mentioned a dog. Yet his text did...

Then another. *Oh, um, me again. Uh, Griffin. I forgot to mention, if you could call me back at this number. It's about a dog.*

I hit redial, and whoever answered, did so with a laugh. "Hello?"

It was the same voice on the voicemails. "Yes, Griffin, is it? I'm returning your call about a dog."

He wasn't laughing now. "Yes. I found a dog. Can you tell me about him?"

What the...? "What? If you found him, then you know what he looks like."

"Yes, but do you?"

Okay, this was officially weird, and after being so damn worried, this random guy was giving me cryptic shit? Almost like he was... "Oh my God. Are you holding him ransom?"

"What? No! I just need to make sure you're his... I mean, this dog's actual owner before I let you take him and use him as bait for dog fights."

I squinted my eyes shut and replayed his words over in my head. Was he accusing me of animal cruelty? Or was he protecting Wicket and making sure I wasn't some sicko like on that episode of—

"Because I watched that episode of 60 *Minutes*," he went on to say. "So you'll have to describe him... I mean, the dog, before I decide if you're legit or not."

I found myself smiling, though I didn't know why. "Yes, it's a he. My number's on his tag, so I'm not sure why you don't think I'm legit, but I'll play along. His name is Wicket. His collar is blue. His favourite food is chicken strips but he'll beg for toast even though he knows he's not allowed to have it. He's a white fluffy thing, looks like an Ewok."

Griffin breathed out a soft laugh. "Hence the name. I figured it had to be a *Star Wars* reference. He looked too much like him for it to be a coincidence."

Oh my God, it was really him. Wicket was found. "Is he okay? Where did you find him?"

"He was at the car park of the National Park. I went there to hike up Mount Coolum, and I have to say, how irresponsible it is to just leave him there without water"

"Mount Coolum?" I barked. "Where the hell is he?"

"I live at Coolum. I found him at the car park at Mount Coolum National Park." Then he was quiet for a second. "Where do you live?"

"I live in Maroochydore, but I'd dropped him off at my parents' house in Caloundra."

"Caloundra?"

"Yes! How the hell did he get from Caloundra to Coolum?"

"I don't know. Maybe he hitched a ride with someone by mistake. He certainly had no problems getting in my car. I had the door open, and he jumped in and sat up in the passenger side like he'd booked an Uber."

"Oh man." I sighed and squeezed my thumb and forefinger into the bridge of my nose. "He likes cars."

"I actually found him yesterday. I hiked yesterday, and I sat at the picnic tables because it was so stinkin' hot. He was there then. I gave him a drink of water, thinking his owners were walking along one of the trails. But then I went back today. I didn't know they close the trail after rain because I'm just new here—well, I'd read it but I just forgot—but Wicket was still there, hiding under one of the tables. He was soaked and muddy. If I hadn't seen him the day before, I wouldn't have thought it was the same dog."

"Oh my God, is he okay?"

"He is now. I gave him a bath and food. He slept like a log."

"You did all that?"

"Of course I did." He sounded indignant. I didn't mean to question his compassion. "And I didn't know he was actually white. Even yesterday before the rain and mud, he was kinda brown. I'd say he's had quite the adventure."

I frowned, my heart heavy knowing Wicket had been through an ordeal. "Where is he now?"

"With me. We're at the beach. He's having a lovely time chasing soldier crabs."

He took him to the beach?

"I was going to take him to the dog park, but I wasn't sure if his vaccinations were up to date..."

"Oh, um..." He'd thrown me for a loop. "Yes, they are. He goes to the vet every six months. Look, he can open screen doors if they're not locked, and that's how he escaped from Mum and Dad's place. Mum doesn't have a licence and Dad can't drive right now. Everyone's been worried sick. My mum keeps crying because she feels responsible. She knows he's like my baby, and I'm stuck on the Gold Coast. I feel so helpless..."

I didn't know why I felt the need to explain all this, but I needed him to know I wasn't a bad person.

His tone was softer now. "Well, he's fine now. You can stop worrying."

I scrubbed my hand over my face. "Thank you. And it is a relief to know he's safe." But now logistics were my biggest issue. "I'm just not sure how I'm going to collect him. I can call one of the local vets to see if they can board him until I get home, I guess. Or maybe a boarding kennel..."

"How long are you away for?" he asked.

"I'm stuck at a work course for another four days."

"I can keep him for four days," Griffin suggested.

"No, I couldn't ask you to do that."

"Why not?"

"Because he's not your responsibility. And you've already done enough, more than I can ever thank you for."

"It's been no problem. I've actually enjoyed it. It's a good excuse to get outside, and my landlady doesn't mind at all. In fact, she thinks he's cute." There was a muffled sound as if he was talking to somebody else, or maybe to Wicket. The wind had picked up and I couldn't make out what he said.

"Sorry, what was that? I couldn't hear you."

There was the sound of panting, like he was running, then laughter, and the sound of the wind stopped dead. I imagined he found shelter wherever he was. The truth was I have no clue where he was, and for that matter, where Wicket was.

"Sorry," Griffin replied breathily. "Had to chase him a bit. He's fast."

"Yeah, he is." I narrowed my eyes. "I don't mean to sound rude or ungrateful... How do I know he's okay?"

"I can send you a photo," he replied simply.

"Oh, um... sure. That'd be great, thanks."

"I meant what I said before. I can look after him, it's really no problem. I do start my new job the day after tomorrow, but the yard at my place is secure. Plus, my landlady will keep an eye on him during the day."

"You live with your landlady?"

He snorted. "No, she converted her house into two. I live upstairs. And I'll be home by dinner time, so I can walk him and give him dinner."

I smiled at that. "It sounds like he's got you wound around his little finger."

He laughed and it was a lovely sound, like happiness and sunshine, and it made my heart warm. "I think he knows it too," Griffin said. "You know, he really does actually smile? I never thought that was something dogs could do, but he does. Like he understands every word I'm saying to him and he just smiles along."

Now it was my turn to laugh. "Oh yeah, he totally does."

I don't know how it happened, but I found myself wondering about this Griffin guy. His voice was warm and smooth and he was obviously kind and compassionate... Maybe he was just a good Samaritan and our paths would never cross again after I got Wicket back, but I was intrigued, that was for sure.

"Okay, look," I said. "If you're sure it's no trouble..."

"No trouble at all," he replied. Then he spoke away from the phone, but I heard him just fine. "Did you hear that, Wicket? Daddy says you can stay a bit longer." Then his voice was back on the phone. "He's smiling."

I chuckled, and for some strange reason, I blushed. "I'm sure he is."

"Okay, well, I'll send you a photo so you know he's fine." A pause. "Uh, what's your name?"

"Oh, Dane. Dane Hughes."

"Well, Dane, Dane Hughes," he replied. I rolled my eyes at his cheesiness but hadn't stopped smiling yet. "I'm Griffin Burke."

"Thank you, Griffin Burke, for being so kind to Wicket."

"You're welcome. And I'm not saying I wouldn't have rescued him if his name wasn't Wicket, but I'm a *Star Wars* fan so it was a no-brainer. Well, that, and the fact he wouldn't get out of my car."

I snorted. "Sorry if he made a mess. Hey, if you wanna send me a PayPal address or something, I can send you some money for his food. I don't expect you to have to pay for anything."

"It's fine. Really, it's no trouble. Like I said, it's been a great excuse for me to get out and explore the coast. I've only been here a few days."

There was so much I wanted to ask him, but someone from the course I was attending signalled me that people were heading back inside for the afternoon session. Shit. I hadn't even had any lunch.

"Well, if you're sure. We can work all that out later anyway," I said. "I gotta go. My course is about to start."

"Well, have fun. We're off to spend the afternoon at Noosa. I'm sure there's a café up there that sells doggie cookies."

I barked out a laugh. "There is." God, what did I say now? "Well, um, stay in touch."

"Will do."

The line went silent and I quickly sent my mum a text. *Wicket's been found. He's in Coolum! Will explain later tonight.*

An hour later as the guest speaker droned on, my stomach rumbled and my attention waned, my thoughts kept going back to Griffin. I carefully snuck out my phone and saw I had three messages, my mum saying, *Thank God!*

Then there were two photos. One was of Wicket, all white and clean and fluffy, sitting on the sandy grass, his bright eyes looking straight up at the camera. And yes, he was smiling. I could also see half of two bare feet in the grass. Griffin's feet, obviously, given that he'd taken and sent the photo.

The grass looked soft and the bare feet reminded me that he was out at the beach and I was stuck in a classroom hearing about optic cabling and broadband restrictions. And that Griffin had nice toes.

The second photo was also of Wicket, this time he was sitting on what looked like an outdoor café chair. God help me. He was actually sitting on the chair at the table. There was a milkshake of some kind on the table in front of the photographer, Griffin, and a plate with a bone-shaped cookie in front of Wicket.

Wicket was grinning.

I laughed in the middle of the guest speaker's talk, then pretended to cover it with a cough. Though I'm sure my smile gave me away. I waited until people stopped looking at me, then thumbed a reply.

He looks so happy, thank you.

Griffin replied. *You're welcome.*

I've been so worried about him. Thank you for taking him home.

My pleasure. He's an absolute joy.

I was going to reply that Wicket was a hole-digging, Steve McQueen escape artist but didn't want to ruin the moment. Instead, I replied, *Feel free to keep me updated on the Griffin and Wicket adventures.*

LOL I will.

"Mr Hughes," the guest speaker said. I looked up, horrified at being busted. "Somewhere else you'd rather be?"

Actually, yes. At Noosa having milkshakes with some pretty cool stranger who picked up my lost dog, who, right this second, is giving him a bone-shaped cookie and taking him on adventures up and down the Sunshine Coast.

I didn't say that, of course. I opted for a more professional response. "Ah, no sir. Sorry for the interruption."

CHAPTER THREE

GRIFFIN

WICKET FELL asleep in the car on the drive home. I took my time winding down David Low Way, taking in the spectacular view of the Pacific Ocean, and my mind kept going over the conversation I'd had with Dane.

He certainly didn't intend to cause harm to Wicket. In fact, he sounded relieved that Wicket was found, safe and well. More than relieved, he even sounded a little choked up. Then we kind of got chatting and I realised that Dane was a nice guy who'd lost his dog.

His voice was easy to listen to, and his laughter warm and throaty; a pleasant sound that I could imagine hearing up close and personal, lips pressed to my ear. I tried not to let my thoughts go down that path. I knew nothing of him, only that he worked in a job that meant he had week-long conferences and his mum babysat his dog. And he had one helluva cute dog.

I pulled up into the garage and Wicket shook himself awake. I waited for him to do his business on the grass, then took him upstairs where he proceeded to plop himself on the couch and go straight back to sleep.

I stood there and watched him, thinking, *lucky bastard,* and wishing I could join him. Then I realised there was no reason why I couldn't join him. So I did. I edged in beside him and lay down. I shoved a cushion under my head and considered closing my eyes for just a minute.

I woke up an hour later when Wicket stretched out against me. Sometime in the last hour, he'd snuggled in beside me, though now he was awake but quite content to just lie there. I smiled at him and rustled the fur between his ears. His tail thumped on the sofa. "Hey, little guy," I said.

He leapt onto the floor, stretched, and shook himself out, then walked over to the door.

"Okay then, point taken," I said, rolling off the couch and letting him outside. He trotted down the stairs and I followed. He was happy to sniff and explore the yard and garden beds, and I was happy to just watch. There was probably an hour of daylight left, and there was a golden sheen to everything the sun touched. Bugs flittered across the top of the garden. The air was still warm.

It was kind of perfect.

"Tomorrow's our last day of freedom," I told Wicket. "What are we gonna do?"

"Get yourself checked for speaking to animals," Bernice said behind me. "Well, speaking to 'em's okay, but asking questions and expecting replies is where it gets shady."

I chuckled, and when I turned, I realised she wasn't alone. She was sitting at her patio table in the shade, beer bottle in her hand. The man who was with her looked to be in his sixties, or thereabouts. He had long grey hair pulled back into a ponytail and a silver goatee, and he wore old, faded board shorts and a T-shirt he either bought from a vintage retro shop or got brand new from a surf shop thirty years ago. Either way, it was cool. He nodded slowly and smiled.

"Oh, hi," I said, walking over to introduce myself. I offered my hand and he shook it. "I'm Griffin Burke."

His handshake was strong and calloused, his smile wide. "Kirk. I hear you've moved in upstairs."

"Yep. And Bernice has very kindly let me keep this little guy." I motioned to Wicket, who was now nose down, tail up in her flower garden. "Until I found his owner. Which I did today, actually."

"Oh, you did?" Bernice asked. Her eyes looked weird. "Are they coming to get him?"

"Not for another few days, if that's okay. The guy who owns him is from Maroochydore, but he's at a work conference on the Gold Coast. His parents live in Caloundra, which is where Wicket escaped from."

We chatted about that for a while, making small talk about how dogs and cats have been known to travel all over the country looking for their owners.

"Pull up a seat," Kirk said, pushing a patio chair out from the table with his foot. I sat down as Kirk stood up, ducking back inside. He called out, "Who wants a beer?"

Bernice inspected her bottle like it was taking her a while to process his question or wondering why she was holding it. "Yeah, why not. Don't normally have two, but it's a nice afternoon." Then she looked at me expectantly.

I shrugged. "Sure, why not?"

It was then I noticed an ashtray on the table and the butted-out remains of what looked like a joint. Well, that explained the mellow smiles and slow blinks. They were both stoned.

Kirk handed me a beer, which I cracked and took a swig

from to hide my smile. They were both grey-haired hippy stoners.

"So," Kirk said, sitting back down at the table. "What brings you to Coolum?"

"Work. I start at the Emporium day after tomorrow."

"Ah, so that's what you meant by last day of freedom."

"Yep."

"What will you be doing there?" he asked.

"Front reception. I'm the ever-professional smiling guy who checks you in. I just don't look it right now." I gestured to my scruffy three-day growth, messy hair, and casual shirt and shorts. "If you saw me dressed for work, you probably wouldn't recognise me."

"Ah." he nodded wisely. "Me too. Looking at me, you wouldn't think I was an ex-surfer dude who ran his own bazaar shop that sells imported Balinese furniture, tie-dyed clothes, and incense."

I snorted my beer because that was *exactly* what he looked like. My reaction was obviously what he was going for because he grinned and leaned back in his chair, relaxed. Well, stoned.

"So, tell me," Bernice said, pointing her beer bottle at me. "Family, yes, no? Girlfriend? Boyfriend?"

God, if this was a quiz show where pensioners passed around a blunt and interrogated people, I was in the hot seat.

Well, here went nothing. "Family, yes. Mum, Dad, one older sister—she's married with two rug rats. Girl-friend? Never. Boyfriend... not at the moment. Unfor-tunately."

Bernice and Kirk didn't seem the kind to judge anyone for being different, and thankfully they didn't react at all. Bernice took a sip of her beer. "Good, good. Shame you didn't get that removalist's number. The one with the hot arse."

I chuckled. "Yeah, shame."

"You know," Kirk said, pulling on his goatee. "Young Jamie at my shop, I could ask him if he's free next week. Nice boy."

I almost choked on my beer. "Nah, I'm good, thanks."

Bernice squinted at him. "Which one's Jamie?"

Kirk motioned toward the top of his head. "You know. Dreadlocks. Vegan. The one who knows where the best weed is coming from."

"Ah." She nodded slowly, then looked around her garden like she was seeing it for the first time. "Jesus, K. Where the fuck did you get this shit from?"

He chuckled. "Buderim. It's good, huh?"

She squinted at him again. "I'm fucking baked."

I chuckled again and took another mouthful of beer.

Bernice grinned at me. "I like you, kid."

"Uh, thanks. I like you too." I finished my beer and stood up. "I'll do the lawns tomorrow morning."

Bernice made a face. "God. Not too early."

I snorted. "No. Not too early. Thank you for the beer. Kirk, it was nice to meet you."

He held out his hand, which I shook. "Call me K, kid. Most folks do."

"Okay..., K. Uh, thanks again. If you need anything, I'll just be upstairs. Give me a holler."

They both nodded and waved me off. I called Wicket over and we went upstairs where I started to think about dinner. After a long day of sun and walking, I didn't feel much like cooking. I felt like pizza and had an idea. I walked out on the balcony and leaned over. "Hey, I'm gonna order a pizza. Want one?"

Both Bernice and K looked up at me with their reddened eyes and lazy smiles. "Hell yes," K said.

Bernice then looked at K. "Told ya I liked him."

———

AN HOUR LATER, pizzas delivered and demolished, I was back upstairs in my flat. Wicket was fed and dozing happily on his spot on the sofa, and I'd just grabbed a bottle of water from my fridge when my phone buzzed.

I'd left it on the coffee table all afternoon, and when I picked it up, I realised I had two missed calls and five text messages. The first voice message was from Nick. "Hey. How're you settling in? Loved the pic from your hike. You look happy, and I'm glad. The guys said to say hi. Call me sometime."

Yes, he was my ex-boyfriend, but he was still a good friend. His message made me smile. I'd call him back tomorrow sometime.

The next voice message was from Mum. "Hey, love. Let us know how you're going. Love you."

Yeah, I'd have to call her back tonight.

The first text was from Amber, my sister. *Just a quick hello. Hope you're settling in. The kids miss their Uncle Griff. Let us know when we can visit ;)*

The next was from my dad. *Do you start work tomorrow? Or the day after? Just wanted to wish you good luck. And call your mother so she'll stop worrying.*

The next three were from Dane.

Finished the course for the day. Just wanted to say thanks again for picking Wicket up and taking such good care of him. I really appreciate it. Your adventures looked fun— better than where I was, that's for sure.

Then another one sent an hour after his first. *Oh, forgot to tell you that he can't have liver treats. Well, he can have them, but you'll be scrubbing carpets afterwards. If you know what I mean.* There was a poop emoticon and a crying face.

Then his last text, which I'd just got. Sent two hours after his second text. *Hope everything's okay. I'm not weird, I promise. I'm just worried and I miss him. Thanks.*

I smiled at my phone.

I took a quick photo of Wicket, asleep on my sofa, and sent it to Dane. The text bubble appeared to tell me he was replying and I waited for what felt like ages.

Cheeky little bugger. He's so cute though. Thank you.

I was just going to text him back, but maybe the second beer K had given me with our pizza went to my head. I eyed his number for a long second and called him instead. He answered on the second ring. "Hello?"

"Hi," I replied. I sat down next to Wicket. "Thought it'd be easier if I just called." Then I had the horrifying realisation that I was probably interrupting something. "Is that okay? Shit, everything's fine, I promise. It's Griffin, by the way."

He chuckled in my ear. "No, it's fine. I'm alone in my hotel room watching crap on TV."

"Oh, thank God. I mean, not that you're alone. Unless you want to be." I closed my eyes slowly, mortified at the stupid that fell out of my mouth. And kept on falling, apparently. "I mean, not that that's any of my business. I just wanted to let you know that Wicket's fine and I didn't think you were a weirdo for texting me. Even though you're probably now wondering the same about me. I didn't mean to worry you; we were just downstairs having pizza with my landlady. I forgot my phone."

He was quiet a second, then barked out a laugh. "I didn't think you were a weirdo."

"Until now, right?"

He chuckled this time. "It's fine. I reckoned you might have thought three text messages were a bit excessive. I was going to send another one to apologise, but then that would have been four."

"I wouldn't have minded. You miss him, I get that."

He sighed. "I do. I was worried something had happened to him."

"Something did. Some awesome guy found him and they've been having adventures every day. Which is probably why he's zonked out already even after we had a nap this afternoon."

"We?" he asked. "You had a nap with Wicket?"

He sounded amused, and I figured he already thought I was a weirdo. "Well yeah, kinda. He plopped himself onto my couch and did that cute little snoring thing, and I thought, 'you know what? That's not a bad idea.'"

Dane laughed. "That cute little snoring thing... I never thought I'd miss his snoring."

"I can record it for you, if you like," I offered, half joking. "He's right beside me, snoring as we speak. Here, listen." I put the phone near Wicket's face so Dane could hear it. When I put the phone back to my ear, there was silence and I'd wondered if the call had been disconnected.

Then he said, his voice quiet, "Thank you."

"That's okay," I offered. "He really is fine. I'll send you more photos tomorrow. Not sure what we're doing yet, but it'll be something fun."

"I'm jealous."

"What? The course you doing not as fun as going to the

beach or hiking through the rainforest? Or milkshakes and puppacinos at Noosa?"

"Not even close," he replied. "Did you get him a puppacino?"

I snorted. "Of course I did. He had to have something to wash his bone cookie down with." Again, silence, and I thought maybe I'd crossed a line. "It's just froth. It won't hurt him."

"Oh no, that's fine. I just can't believe you did that."

"Why wouldn't I? Just so you know, I spoil my niece and nephew like that too. Drives my sister up the wall, but whatever. I won't get the coolest uncle award by saying no to sugar, will I?"

Now he laughed. "How old are they? Your niece and nephew."

"Three and four. Lane is three, and she's a firecracker, and Bristol's four. He's into dinosaurs at the moment."

"There's a shop in the plaza where I work that has a bunch of dinosaur figures," he said. "They look kinda cool."

"Which plaza is that?"

"Maroochydore Palms."

"Oh, thanks. I'll check it out." Then I thought about that. "I thought you did some corporate job to be away at a week-long work conference."

He made a sound that sounded like a muffled groan. "Well, not really. I'm the store manager of the Telstra shop."

It was weird. He said it as if he was waiting for some snarky reply.

"Cool," I said. "That's pretty impressive."

Again with the hesitation. "Really?"

"Yeah, why wouldn't it be?"

"Well, when I tell people I work for Telstra, most

people either bitch at me for the cost of their phone bills or because their internet crapped out on them."

"But that's not your fault."

He laughed. "Oh my God. You're the sanest person I've ever spoken to."

I snorted at that. "Well, I work front of house for a five-star resort. Well, I used to, in Brisbane. I start my new job day after tomorrow, doing the same thing but a bit higher up. And I can tell you, when people are paying big dollars, that comes with big expectations. And rightly so. But when things go wrong, as they sometimes do, they want someone to blame. It's not personally my fault that they expected the room service menu to be free, but it's my job to resolve any issues. I need to make the customer happy while keeping the integrity of the hotel in check. Still doesn't mean they're gonna get free room service."

Dane laughed again. "I should totally use that tomorrow in our Customer Service Resolution segment."

"By all means, feel free."

"Do people really expect room service to be included?"

I scoffed. "You work in customer service, right?"

"Point taken."

I found myself smiling. "It's crazy, isn't it?"

"Sure is." It sounded like he changed which ear he had his phone pressed to. "So, your new job is a promotion?" he asked. "It's just... you said it was a step up."

"Yeah. It'll be a bit of a challenge, but I'm looking forward to it. And plus, in my time off I get to hang out at the beach and go hiking. I might even learn how to surf."

"You like the outdoors. I mean, from your adventures with Wicket, you're the adventurous type. Most people plant their arse in front of the TV."

"Well, I do my fair share of arse-planting." I froze, then panicked. "Um, that kind of sounded wrong."

Dane barked out a laugh so loud Wicket woke up and looked around the room.

"Hey," I said before Dane could reply about my arse-planting comment. "Wicket heard your laugh. I think he's looking for you. Say his name, talk to him and I'll put the phone near his ear."

I put my phone near Wicket's little face and I could hear the tinny mumble of Dane saying something, but I couldn't work out the words exactly. Wicket cocked his head to the side, his ears perked up, and his eyes went wide. "He's listening!" I said, hoping Dane would hear me.

When Wicket tried to lick my phone, I pulled it back and put it to my ear. Then I heard what Dane was saying. "...just hold on, little buddy, I'll come and get you soon. I know you're probably having fun and I hope he's looking after you okay. I miss you and Grandma was really sad you ran away."

It was so damn sweet. He used a cutesy voice to talk to him, and I had to wonder just who this Dane guy really was. It was pretty obvious we could talk without effort, and we seemed to have a lot in common... except I had no clue if he was gay or bi, or remotely interested, or even single. And as he spoke to his dog over the phone, I felt like I was intruding, and my heart squeezed because Dane was obviously missing his dog. Then I felt guilty for smiling at the cuteness because, at the end of the day, Dane was sad and there was nothing cute about that.

"He tried to lick my phone," I said quietly. "But he definitely heard you. He was looking at the phone, doing that cute head-tilt thing."

Dane sighed. "Yeah. Thanks."

"Well, I better let you go," I said. "I don't know what adventures we're going on tomorrow yet, but I'll be sure to send photos."

"Yeah, that'd be great." It sounded like he was smiling now.

"Okay, well, have fun at your boring customer service complaint course tomorrow."

He groaned. "Ugh. Don't remind me. But if Wicket demands another trip to a café and orders a puppacino, keep a tab for me so I can pay you back."

I chuckled. "Yeah, it's totally his idea."

He was quiet for a second. "Night."

"Goodnight."

I hit End Call and slid my phone into my pocket. I hadn't realised it had gotten so late. I guessed we talked longer than I thought. It was weird though. I was left with an unsettled feeling; one I couldn't quite identify. This guy, that I didn't even know, felt like shit because I had his dog. I mean, I rescued his dog and he was grateful, but he missed him nonetheless. And I liked that we could chat so easily. Even if he wasn't inclined to be interested, maybe we could still be friends. I needed to make new friends here, and Dane seemed like a good place to start. I mean, it wasn't as if I could ask him if he was straight without sounding like a creep.

Wicket was sitting up on the sofa beside me now, and when I pulled out my phone, he stood up and peered at it, probably trying to see if he could hear Dane's voice again. I snapped a quick photo and sent it to Dane, adding, *Wicket says goodnight.*

His reply came through a few minutes later. *Night, little buddy.*

Oh, the *little buddy* part made my heart sink and fly at

the same time. I was getting a little too invested, too soon. Okay, so maybe I couldn't ask him outright if he was interested, but I could ask him what the bar scene was like or mention Grindr or the word 'ex-boyfriend' in passing, or maybe I could just man the fuck up and tell him I was gay and see what his reaction was.

Yeah, I thought sarcastically. *Because that's always ended well.*

CHAPTER FOUR

DANE

THE PHOTO of Wicket on Griffin's sofa kind of hurt to see, I couldn't lie. There he was, so far away from me, with someone else. And it was stupid, really, but I felt like a dad whose kid had gone to school on the first day and I was left behind while they were being all grown-up.

Like I said. It was stupid.

But then I noticed something else in the photo.

Wicket was sitting up on a brown leather sofa, his front foot on Griffin's thigh. Wicket's eyes were big, brown, and curious, looking at the phone as the photo was taken, and like Griffin said, his head was tilted in that cute way he did. He looked happy and healthy enough, safe and well-fed. None of that was a concern to me.

Griffin had his free hand on Wicket's side, probably patting him or giving him a scratch, and that was all fine too.

But he wore a bracelet that caught my eye. A dark leather bracelet that had a small silver clasp with small bands of colour. The gay pride colours, to be exact.

My heart did some weird, tight-skipping-swoop thing. He could have been oblivious to the whole rainbow pride thing, though I was pretty certain that particular bracelet was only for sale on LGBT sites. Which meant one thing. He was LGBT, or somewhere on the LGBT spectrum. Maybe.

Okay then.

Jesus, Dane. Get a grip.

It didn't mean anything. I didn't know if he was single or even looking or even remotely interested. The fact I could talk to him like no one else didn't mean anything either. Just because he understood my job didn't make me the poster child for everything right and wrong in the telecommunications industry. I loved my job, and I hated that it became an issue when brought up in conversation with some people.

But not Griffin.

He understood the whole concept of being the face of a brand was wanting our customers to be happy. Sure, guys were okay with it only after I'd explained it, but Griffin got it from the get-go.

And he was so kind to Wicket. Above everything else, that's what I liked the most. He didn't just treat him like a dog. He treated him exactly the way I did.

Jesus, Dane. Get a grip.

I told myself that a hundred times; getting ready for bed, lying in bed. Even in my dreams, dream-me told me to get a grip. I was slipping down a slope of puppacino froth and my brain kept telling me to *get a damn grip, Dane. Just get a goddamn grip.* I woke up with a start, just before my alarm went off. I had a shower, got dressed, forced some breakfast down, all the while telling myself to get a bloody grip.

And I kind of did, until the first message made my phone beep just after nine a.m. It was a photo, of course. Of a now-slightly-green Wicket rolling in fresh grass clippings. Those grass stains weren't coming out of his fur anytime soon, but the smile on his face was ridiculous.

There was a laughing emoticon and a caption. *Little bugger. Good thing he's cute.*

I couldn't reply because we were in the middle of open discussions, though I was sure a few people noticed I was sneaking a look at my phone. Either that or my smile gave me away.

About an hour later, my phone buzzed again. Another photo. This time, a very wet Wicket was standing on a boogie board, floating in ankle deep water with Griffin's bracelet hand holding the board. Wicket's tongue was hanging out the side of his mouth, and it looked like he was smiling up at, not the camera exactly, but more at Griffin.

A caption followed it. *Swim and surfing lesson 1:Grass stains* o

Was it absurd that, along with missing Wicket like crazy, I was also feeling a bit jealous? Not of Griffin getting to spend time with my dog. But of Wicket getting to spend time with Griffin. I couldn't help but think it was unfair that Wicket knew what Griffin looked like and I didn't.

Jesus, Dane. Get a grip.

This was getting ludicrous, but the more I didn't want Griffin to send me any more photos, the more I couldn't wait.

And he didn't disappoint.

They were at the beach. Coolum Beach, if I could tell correctly. The photo was of a sleeping Wicket on a beach towel, flat out on his back, his little feet in the air. He usually slept that way when he'd had a busy day... but he was kind of lying against Griffin. Well, I assumed it was Griffin. Lean, a little pale, I could see a glimpse of skin above his bunched-up blue board shorts, then long legs with dark leg hair and long feet, then a stretch of golden sand and white-capped waves on the aqua blue ocean.

The caption read *Battery recharge complete in 4... 3... 2...*

The scenery, one of the world's most beautiful beaches, paled in comparison to the body shot. It wasn't even provocative in any way. He didn't send the photo of him. He sent it of Wicket, sound asleep after a fun morning doing crazy things. But I couldn't stop looking at him. At Griffin, that is. His skin looked cool from the water and warmed by the sun. I could see a dusting of salt and sand, and his thigh looked lean but strong and defined. His feet... he had really big feet, and those too-cute toes I'd seen in an earlier photo of him barefoot in the grass...

God, I was in trouble.

How was that even possible? I didn't even know this guy. Well, I did, a little bit, but not really. I felt like I knew him. That with every photo, with every caption, I got to see the real him. I'd spoken to him, sure. And from our few phone conversations, I knew he was passionate about the welfare of animals, worked front desk at five-star hotels, lived upstairs from an old lady and mowed her lawn, and had a sense of humour. I knew he loved being outdoors, loved being active, ate pizza, and took naps in the afternoon because my dog did and he thought it looked like a great idea.

I knew enough, and I knew that, yeah, I was in trouble.

By lunchtime, I had another photo. It was Wicket in the passenger side of what I assumed to be Griffin's car. Griffin was standing next to his car, the door open. Wicket was standing on the seat with a grin on his little face and a look that kind of said, *Would you hurry the hell up?*

The caption said, *He's impatient. I said 'puppacino' and he started to bounce.* He'd tacked on a laughing emoticon, and I was smiling at my phone as I replied.

You're killing me! I'm so jealous but I'm loving the pics. Wish I was with you guys instead of here.

The little text bubble showed, and I got butterflies knowing Griffin's reply was coming. *We had lunch at the Surf Club. We shared grilled fish and chips. Wicket didn't mind the no puppacino because he lo-o-o-o-ves fish! I told him we'd have to do lunch with you when you come to pick him up. Hope you don't mind.*

Don't mind at all. My shout.

Wicket says there better be puppacinos. LOL

Sonia, a manager from Brisbane, nudged my elbow with hers. "Someone was lying the other day when he said he wasn't seeing someone..."

It took me a second to remember our conversation the other night, and I had, indeed, told her I was single.

"No, I'm not. I promise."

"No one smiles at photos like that to someone they're not into."

I held up my phone and showed her the photo. "It's my dog, Wicket. He's kinda like my kid."

Sonia studied the photo for a second. "He's a cutie. Who's he staying with while you're here?"

"It's kind of a long story, but he's being babysat by a guy in Coolum..."

Sonia's smile was slow-spreading. I imagined it matched mine. She raised her eyebrows. "Yeah, the smile. It's for the guy, not the cute fur baby."

I tried to not smile. "Maybe. I don't know."

Sonia hummed and stabbed her salad with a fork,

shoving it in her mouth to hide the smug smirk. "Mmm, I think you do."

I bit into my sandwich so I didn't have to answer her. Instead, I sent back a text that I regretted sending as soon as I'd done it. *You'll have to send a photo that includes you so I know who I'm meeting in three days...*

———

GRIFFIN HADN'T REPLIED by the time I went back to the afternoon session of my course, and I was pretty sure he now thought I was some freak who was one text away from asking for dick pics. Or sending them.

Regret churned the sandwich in my stomach, and I pretended to be interested in the focus-group stuff I was supposed to be taking part in. Yet, I couldn't stop thinking about Griffin, and the other relationships I'd messed up or dodged a bullet on.

I'd had my fair share of broken hearts, and I'd done my share of the breaking. The longest relationship I'd had was twelve months, and instead of celebrating our one-year anniversary going out for dinner and having incredible sex, Tamir collected his few things from my place and told me he was sorry.

His family would never accept his *inclination for men* and it would be better for everyone if he were to end things and leave.

Sure, he'd broken my heart, but I didn't hold it against him. He wasn't ready to come out because of his overly religious family and would probably never be able to. I would never begrudge anyone for not being out. Everyone had their reasons, and not everyone was as lucky as me to have a completely accepting family.

That was over a year ago, and apparently my heart was vying for new attention. It had certainly taken an interest in Griffin, a guy I'd barely known for a few days, whether my brain thought it was a good idea or not. It wasn't anything more than infatuation; at least my brain could rein my heart in that much. But infatuation was still enough to make me a little giddy and nervous, and then I remembered that Griffin was probably considering driving Wicket to a vet and letting them look after him until I could collect him because I'd requested a photo like it would determine whether I wanted to have lunch with him in three days...

Nope. I couldn't think of that right now.

I let my memories wander on their own and tried to recall the relationships I'd had before Tamir. There'd been a healthy share of one-nighters and the occasional two-nighters and a few guys I'd dated a month or so.

But no one who had caught my eye or connected with me in any way. I needed a connection over anything else because, if I connected with a guy, attraction followed. Sure, I'd seen guys I'd been in lust with, who I thought were hot as hell as soon as I saw them. But if I couldn't talk to them, hold a conversation, and chat with them, my heart wasn't in it.

Tamir and I had first met when he'd come into the store. There was nothing more than held gazes and timid smiles; it was a professional transaction, after all. But then I'd run into him the next week at an outdoor concert with my friends, and after a second of mutual trying to place each other, we joined the dots to his new phone and his visit to the Telstra shop.

It had been slow between us at first, while Tamir found his feet, and it was secretive. But I didn't mind. I liked him, and we were never short on conversation. I didn't even mind the not-going-out or the no-PDA rules or the fact his family didn't even know I existed. I understood his dilemma; it wasn't an ideal situation for either of us. But behind closed doors, things had been easy and natural, until it wasn't. For him, anyway. But like I said, I didn't blame him. I was over it now, and like my mum had said after I'd told her Tamir left me and she'd hugged me and cried with me, I'd find someone else who would make me happy. When my heart was healed and ready, she'd said, I'd find someone, more than likely, when I wasn't even looking.

Well, I wasn't looking now. I really wasn't.

Or so I told myself.

And when Griffin still hadn't replied when I was back in my hotel room for the night, disappointment fought with regret in my belly. It was stupid, really. That I should be tied up in knots over a guy I barely knew. We'd had no more contact than a few phone calls, a couple of laughs, and a bunch of text messages. And the photos. Let's not forget the photos.

Sonia had insisted I meet with her and the rest of the gang in the hotel restaurant at seven, and truth be told, I didn't have much of an appetite. But this work conference was about networking as much as it was educational and about team building, and so I'd agreed.

I changed into jeans and a T-shirt, put on some more deodorant, splashed my face with water, and told my reflection in the bathroom mirror to get his shit together. Everyone was at the bar when I arrived an artful ten minutes late. One beer and a few laughs later, I was feeling much better. I'd managed to not think, or overthink, as tended to be my problem, about things I couldn't control and settled in to have a good night with some work friends.

When we were sitting at our table waiting for our meals,

Jamie was telling a funny story about a customer who had brought in their laptop because of internet connectivity issues only to discover, in a very public setting, that it was the illegal downloading of porn that had infected his device with viruses.

We'd all burst into laughter just as my phone beeped with a message. It was from Griffin, and I braced myself for a short, terminating text.

Busy afternoon. Going for walks and taking naps, you know, the important stuff. He added a wink.

Then followed with a photo, and I almost dropped my phone. It was a selfie of a dark-haired guy with a bit of scruff, wearing sunglasses and a breathtaking smile. He was holding Wicket, and I didn't know which of them was grinning the biggest. The sun was shining, they were outside, trees in the background, so possibly a park or a backyard.

My heart squeezed, uncomfortably tight and wonderful at the same time. Griffin was... well, he was... I stared at the picture. I couldn't look away. If someone said, design your idea of a perfect guy, I was staring at it. Gorgeous, smiling in the sunshine, and holding Wicket. That was the holy trifecta.

"What is it?" Sonia asked, trying to peek at my phone screen.

"Oh, nothing, sorry," I said. I hadn't realised the conversation around the table had stopped and they were looking at me.

"Is that him?" Sonia asked, her smile wide and knowing.

I let out a long breath and handed her my phone. She stared at it, then stared at me. "I can see why you're reconsidering your single status. He's cute!"

"I'm not reconsidering anything," I said, not sounding one bit convinced.

I was saved by the waiter bringing our dinner, thankful for the distraction. Everyone was trying not to look at me and pretended I wasn't blushing. Sonia slid my phone to me and gave me a kind smile. She leaned in and whispered, "Sorry."

"It's fine." I took a deep breath and shook my head, turning my plate around. "I, um, it's only kind of new, and he doesn't know..." God, my face flamed.

Mack, a guy from Townsville, gave me a pointed look. "Did you learn nothing from today's focus group on risk management having a positive outcome?"

I snorted. "All I learned today was that my dog is having the time of his life with the man of my dreams, and I'm stuck here with you guys."

Mack laughed. "I'll give you the short version of what was a three-hour lecture. Take the risk."

They all smiled, and one by one, they raised their glasses. "Cheers to that."

CHAPTER FIVE

I'D DELIBERATELY SENT Dane a photo of Wicket that included my hand with the bracelet, and he never mentioned the bracelet at all. Maybe he didn't know what it was. Maybe he was straight and happily paired off with some super nice girl. Hell, he could be married for all I knew.

After all, straight guys rarely noticed wristbands, let alone one with a small silver clasp with even smaller bands of colour. But someone in the know definitely would notice it, and as it turned out, Dane was obviously not.

I was a little disappointed. I couldn't help but wish this newfound back-and-forth banter with him was going somewhere, and there'd been mention of a lunch date in a few days. But after he never commented about the stupid bracelet, I was pretty sure I was heading up a dead-end street.

I spent the rest of the afternoon enjoying my last day of freedom by taking another quick nap—at Wicket's insistence—then a long walk to the park. Also at Wicket's insistence. Then I made sure my work uniform was all in order, set about making some dinner, and finally replied to Dane.

I hadn't ignored him deliberately. Like I said, I was busy. And disappointed. But then he'd asked for a photo of me, so he knew who he was taking out for lunch. It wasn't a date, I reminded myself. He was just being polite after I'd rescued Wicket. That was all. Who knew, maybe he'd bring his girlfriend along...

I wasn't sure what the photo request was really about though. Was it a security thing? So he could give the photo to his family to provide to the police should he never be seen again? Hell, maybe that wasn't such a bad idea.

Not that I thought he was some crazy axe murderer or psycho catfisher, but I also wasn't naïve. 'He met up with some random man' was usually how segments of *Australia's Most Wanted* started, and let's be honest. Most people thought *how could he have been so stupid?* when they heard news reports of people wandering off to meet someone they met online or over the phone.

And I wasn't naïve, but I still liked to believe there are good people in the world. I liked to think there were still people who were who they said they were. But I needed to be smart about the whole thing. I'd meet him in a public place to hand Wicket back, and I'd tell someone where I was going. But having a photo of him wouldn't hurt. That was even if he would send me an actual real photo and not some profile picture he'd stolen from some unsuspecting guy online.

I sighed loud enough that Wicket looked up at me from eating his dinner. "Is your dad a good guy?" I asked him. Which was stupid. I didn't think anyone who loved a dog as much as Dane seemed to could be a horrible person. And him asking for a photo wasn't totally unreasonable, I allowed. If it was for security reasons. I mean, it wasn't like he was interested and wanted to know what I looked like for interested reasons.

Was it?

Would me asking him for a photo be for security reasons or to quench my own curiosity?

Would he send me an honest photo, or would he lie? I'd find out in three days if it was or wasn't him that turned up to collect Wicket... I mean, what if it wasn't Wicket's owner at all?

An unease crept over me. I really should see who I was expecting to pick up Wicket. I mean, Wicket's reaction to seeing him would be answer enough, but I should have a visual too, right? Not just for my own security, but for Wicket's too, right?

Absolutely.

I scrolled through the photos I'd taken this afternoon and found one of me and Wicket at the park. It was a selfie and it was a half-decent shot of me, so taking a deep breath, I attached the pic and hit Send.

Now, how to ask for one in return without sounding like a creeper, or a Grindr pick-up line...

Man, I sucked at this.

Then my phone beeped with a reply message from Dane. *Great photo. Wicket looks so happy. He won't want to come home with me.* He added the cross-eyed emoticon which made the tone of his text more sarcastic-truth than sad-truth.

He didn't mention me being in the photo at all in his comment, so he was either straight or not interested because, surely another gay or bi or remotely curious guy would notice the guy holding a dog in a photo.

Or maybe that was just me...

My phone pinged with a follow-up message. *Just out for dinner with friends. Sonia's not sure which of you is cuter.* Then he added a crying-laughing emoticon, which could mean one of two things: he thought that was hilarious because obviously his dog was cuter than another dude. Or, he was testing the water by kind-of, in a second-hand way, calling me cute. Or maybe there was a third thing by saying a woman found me cute and that was his way of seeing how I reacted. I really had no clue, but one thing was certain. This felt like a test.

And he'd shown my photo to his friends, and that could possibly mean a dozen different things I wasn't sure I wanted to analyse right then.

I thumbed out a reply. *Tell Sonia I said thanks... I think.* ;)

Then I realised my reply gave as much away as his texts did, but I didn't know what to add without sounding lame. I needed to somehow ask for a photo, also without sounding lame.

This was becoming far too complicated.

Wicket walked to the door and looked over at me expectantly. I let him outside and followed him down the stairs so he could pee, poop, or sniff, or whatever important work he needed to do. I sat on the second bottom step while he wandered off and I stared at my phone.

"Don't look so worried. It might never happen," Bernice said from her patio table, scaring the crap outta me.

I put my hand to my heart. "Jesus."

"My friends call me Bernice."

I barked out a laugh and walked over, taking a seat at her table. "I didn't see you there."

"Just enjoying a cup of tea and a medicinal brownie

before bed." She nodded to the plate where half a hash brownie still sat. "Helps me sleep. Want some?"

"Nah. I start work tomorrow. Last thing I need is a random drug test to get me fired before I start. Thanks for the offer though."

"Is that what you're worried about?"

"No, work's fine." I sighed. "Wicket's owner is..." I struggled to finish that sentence and settled on another sigh.

"He's what? An asshole? In jail?"

I snorted. "No, nothing like that. He's... well, I don't know what he is."

"What do you mean? You're gonna need to spell it out for me, son. I'm a little blitzed."

I studied her more closely, and yeah, her eyes were doing that slow-blinking thing. "I don't know if he's... interested."

"Ah." She nodded wisely. "Well, you can do one of two things. You can *not* ask him and die wondering. Or you can do what grown-ups do and be grown-up about it and ask him outright. Like a grown-up."

"It's not that easy."

"Yes, it is."

"What if he's not?"

"Then you'll know he's not. End of story."

I sighed again because that right there was the problem. I didn't want it to be the end of this or our story.

Bernice popped the rest of the brownie in her mouth, chewed, and swallowed it while watching me, waiting for me to reply. When I didn't, she sighed like she was all out of patience. And out of brownie. "But Griffin, what if he is interested?"

My stomach clenched. "Well, I—"

My phone beeped, cutting me off. It was a message

from Dane… No, not just a message. It was a photo. It was kinda dark, like there was mood lighting in what looked like a restaurant. There was a guy wearing a dark grey Hurley shirt and sitting at a table alongside the cropped-out-of-view shoulder of a blonde girl. He had short brown hair, blue eyes that reflected the light, and pink lips. He looked like he was smiling shyly, maybe blushing a little. He reminded me oddly of Stephen Amell, in a very, very good way.

"Holy shit," I mumbled.

"What's that?" Bernice asked.

"He just sent me a photo."

"Of what?"

"Of himself."

She didn't ask to see the picture, and guessing from how her eyes were now nothing but slits, I wasn't surprised.

"Well, there's your answer," she said.

"My answer to what?"

"Whether he's interested."

I made a face that she could either not see or didn't care about. Possibly both. "How so?"

"He didn't just send a photo," she said, her words slow. "He put his cards on the table, that's what he did."

"I sent him my photo first."

"Then you put your cards on the table first."

I wasn't sure if she was dead wrong or very right.

"Griffin," she said, slow blinking. "He's interested. No one sends their photo to anyone else unless they're interested. Fact's a fact."

"Maybe."

"If he was married with two kids, would he be sending photos to a guy?"

"Well, yeah, if he was unfaithful. And bi."

"And interested. Cause I'm telling ya, if he was a

straight guy who wasn't the least bit interested, he wouldn't be sending no photo of himself to another guy."

Then another message beeped. It was Dane. *Sonia said it was only fair you know what I looked like too.*

My heart was hammering. "His friend said it was only fair I know what he looked like as well."

"Because he's interested."

I was starting to think he was. I couldn't stop staring at him...

"Is he handsome?"

"He's fucking beautiful."

Bernice laughed. "Then hurry up and reply."

Then it occurred to me... "Oh God. I have to reply?"

She snorted and swayed a little. "Jesus, go upstairs and do it. I'm going to bed while I still got my buzz on. Am I still dog-sitting tomorrow?"

"Yeah, is that okay?"

"Sure is." She stood up and swayed again, but like she was long-used to it, she drifted inside and slid the glass door closed behind her. I heard the lock click into place and made sure Wicket had done his business before we went back upstairs.

I parked my arse on the sofa, and taking a deep breath, I replied. *So, do you do all your own stunt work on your TV show* Arrow?

I hit Send before I could change my mind, and his reply came back almost immediately.

My what?

Oh shit. *Is that photo really of you, or is it Stephen Amell? Or are you really Stephen Amell?*

I waited for thirty heart-stopping seconds before the reply text bubble appeared. Then disappeared, then reappeared, then disappeared again. Then my phone rang, almost causing my heart to leap out of my chest.

"I had to google who that was," he said instead of hello.

Hoping I sounded calm, I asked, "You've never heard of Stephen Amell?"

He snorted. "I recognised the pictures online when I googled him, but I don't watch the show."

"Has no one ever told you that you look like him?"

"Ah, no."

And Bernice's words came back to me. *Just be a grown-up and ask him outright.* I let out a breath as steady as what I could make it. "Can I ask you something?"

"Sure."

Aaaaand then I chickened out. Then I panicked. "What do you do on a Thursday night at eight-thirty if you don't watch Stephen Amell in *Arrow* on TV?"

He laughed quietly. "Probably walk the dog or have dinner... No wait, eight-thirty on a Thursday night is *The Walking Dead*."

"Oh, hell no. I watched the first episode of the first season and almost died."

He laughed. "It's good!"

"It's horrifying!"

"Is that really what you were going to ask me?"

"No," I answered before my brain could catch up. *That was me, honest to a fault.* Jesus Christ. "Oh. Um, yeah, it doesn't really matter..."

"If you want to know something, then it matters."

I closed my eyes and took a deep breath. "How old are you?" Not what I really wanted to know, but it was a start.

"Twenty-six. How old are you?"

"Twenty-four."

"That wasn't what you really wanted to know, was it?" he asked, though it wasn't really a question.

"Well... no."

"Do you want to know if I'm seeing someone?"

"Maybe."

It sounded like he was smiling. "I'm not. Seeing anyone, that is."

Okay, so that was one hurdle down. "And if you were looking—" I cringed at how ridiculous this was. "—and used dating apps, would you use Tinder? Or maybe Grindr?" I buried my face into the sofa cushion and rolled my eyes and wanted to die.

He barked out a laugh. "Are you asking me if I'm gay?"

"Yes."

"What was that?"

I lifted my face from the cushion and tried speaking again. "Yes."

"I am."

My heart went from pounding out a mortified death march to doing some techno rapid-fire staccato. "Yay! Well, I mean, that's good." *I just said yay. Fuck my life.* I cleared my throat and tried again. "And I mean, good, if you like that kind of thing..."

"Do you?" he asked, sounding amused. "Like that kind of thing?"

"Yes."

"I thought so."

That sobered me. Did he assume? Did he think I *sounded* gay? Did he stereotype people before he even met them? Because that kind of pissed me off. "What do you mean you thought so?"

"Your bracelet."

"Oh." I almost laughed. "I forgot about that."

"So you did show it in the photo deliberately?"

"Maybe."

He chuckled. "So... are you on Grindr?"

"No. It's not my thing. You?"

"Nah. My friends tried to get me into it but it's not my thing either. Call me boring, but I like meeting guys the good old-fashioned way."

"The old-fashioned way? Like having your dog run away and hoping some random guy finds him?"

Dane laughed again, a deep throaty sound. "Can't say I planned it, no. But I'm interested to see where it goes."

Holy shit.

I tried to breathe. "Yeah, me too."

"So, you start your new job tomorrow?"

"I do."

"Nervous?"

"A little bit, but I'm sure it'll be fine. Once I get there and meet everyone."

"So you moved up here from Brisbane for this job? A promotion, right?"

"Yeah, kind of. A definite step up anyway."

"Well, that's great. And let's face it, living on the Sunshine Coast isn't exactly terrible."

I snorted. "No, it's not."

"So, this Friday? When I get home, will you be working?"

How could I have forgotten that? "Oh crap. Yes. Until five, anyway. Is that too late? If you want to pick Wicket up earlier, I can organise—"

"No, it's fine. I won't get home till three-ish, so that works out well actually. By the time I get home, start laundry, and maybe pick up a few groceries—you know how that is—I'll need an hour or so before I drive up to get him. Five sounds good."

"So, no lunch then?"

"Dinner could work."

"It could."

"So, where am I meeting you?"

I remembered my online-safety inner monologue from earlier. I did trust him, and I was excited that we'd cleared the air and admitted an interest. But I still needed to be smart about this. "How about we meet at the beach?" I suggested. "That way Wicket gets to have a run, and the surf club has alfresco tables and we can order dinner..." The 'and it's a public place' went unsaid.

"Sounds good."

"It does."

"Okay, I better let you go. You've got a big day tomorrow."

"Yeah."

"For what it's worth, I'm glad we cleared the air tonight."

"Me too."

"I'll give you a call tomorrow night to see how your first day went."

My smile became a grin. "Okay."

"Tell Wicket I said goodnight."

"He's already sound asleep. Curled up beside me on the couch."

Dane made a deep sigh sound that could have been a moan. It made me shiver.

"Goodnight, Griffin."

"Night, Dane."

The line went dead, and I sat there for a good five minutes trying to calm my heart and trying not to get ahead of myself. Something was budding between us, but there was no guarantee it would take hold, let alone grow and bloom.

Don't get ahead of yourself. Don't read too much into this. Don't have expectations...

I was still holding my phone, so I opened it to Dane's photo and my heart tripped over. The look on his face was a shy smile, like he was looking right at me. He was really very good-looking: defined cheekbones, strong jaw, and kind blue eyes. But more than that, he was a nice guy. And he was gay, and he was interested in seeing where this thing between us went...

I could still hear the echo of his warm laugh in my ear, and I wondered if he was tall or not, if he had tattoos. I wondered what his favourite food was, what he couldn't stand. Which colour was his favourite, what he smelled like, what his hands felt like.

Don't get ahead of yourself.

Yeah right. Good luck with that.

———

I ARRIVED for my first day at work twenty minutes early. I hadn't slept all too well, too excited and nervous to sleep, so after making sure Bernice had everything for Wicket's first day with her, I found myself making introductions to my new boss.

Her name was Neda Husak. She was a middle-aged woman, thin, with a straight back and a certain poise that said she was approachable but had no time for bullshit. And whether she was pleased with my being early or expected nothing less, I wasn't sure. I'd met her during the interview process, and she came across then as an astute businesswoman who expected nothing less than the best at all times. I was pretty sure we were going to get along just fine.

She clapped her hands together and said, "Excellent. Follow me."

And then I didn't have time to be excited or nervous. Her method of induction was clearly *the tell me, show me, let me* method, followed by the *sink or swim* method.

I was fine with both.

It helped that the computer system was the same I'd used at my last job, so at least I could hit the ground running. I was the newest of the hotel's three reception managers and I met a good portion of the front-of-house staff. Some I would answer to; some would answer to me.

And outside of work, taking a dog for a run on the beach, I could be a twenty-four-year-old guy without a care in the world. But at work, in uniform, I was the utmost professional. Clean shaven, hair styled perfectly, and ever-smiling, I greeted each and every person like I was their personal attendant.

As far as first days went, it was smooth, and I hoped I made a good impression. I'd barely made it out of the drive of the resort when my phone rang. It was my mum. The call went straight to Bluetooth. "Hi, love. How was it?" she asked.

"Good, I think. My boss likes me, which probably means most of the people I work with don't."

Mum snorted. "That's never stopped you."

"I know. But they were all nice so far."

"Did you make the right decision moving up there?" she asked.

"Yes."

"That's my boy. No hesitation, no regrets."

I rolled my eyes. "If only personal relationships were as easy as professional ones."

"Oh?" She never missed a thing. "Have you met someone already?"

I could picture her having to put her cup of tea down. "Maybe. It's early days. Like really early days, but maybe."

"And what's his name?"

I considered not telling her. Citing it would jinx it all for sure. But it was my mum and I always told her. "His name is Dane. But that's all I'm saying right now."

She made a happy sound. "Okay, okay. I won't ask you anything else. You just be yourself and the right boy will come along, just you watch."

I rolled my eyes. "Yes, Mum."

We said our goodbyes just as I pulled up at home. I got out of my car and quickly made my way to the gate at the backyard. I was dying to see how Wicket and Bernice had gotten on all day. I didn't want to admit I was worried Wicket might have got himself into trouble or escaped because, God, what would I tell Dane then? But I needn't have worried.

I stuck my head around the back of the house, and there was Bernice sitting at her patio table with her bare foot rubbing Wicket's belly. He lay on his back, clearly enjoying the sun and the attention. "Am I interrupting something?" I asked.

Bernice looked up at me and gave me a slow smile. I was pretty sure she was high. It was hard to tell; she was so laid back about everything, I wasn't sure if she was toked up or just chill.

Wicket still hadn't moved. I peered closer. "Is he...?"

"Dead?" Bernice said. "Dead dogs don't snore."

"Is he baked?"

She snorted. "You think I would waste my stash on a dog?"

I laughed and Wicket shot up. Bernice pulled her foot away, and he shook his little body awake. "Hey buddy," I said and was rewarded with a jumpy, happy lick. I gave him a good pat. "How about I go get changed and we go to the park?"

Bernice just kept on smiling. Her eyes were clear so, no, not stoned, just happy. "We've had a good day. He's kept me company while I made some mango jam, and we did some gardening and had afternoon tea. Then the sun made us lazy and we haven't moved since."

"Sounds like a perfect day."

"He has a calming effect on me. I think his little doggie aura puts out good vibes."

I chuckled. "I think it does too."

"How was your first day?"

"Really good."

"Well, you look as polished now as you did this morning. I don't think they're working you hard enough."

I snorted at that and put my hand to my chest and gave her my at-work voice. "Don't be mistaken, ma'am. I look this good all the time."

Her shoulders shook as she laughed. "I'm sure you do. Oh, K'll be coming around later when he shuts up his store. Just in case you see someone coming and going."

"No worries." Wicket was now doing an impatient dance at my feet. "Okay, okay, give me two minutes!"

Our walk to the park consisted of Wicket sniffing everything he could put his nose to and trotting around with his little happy tail in the air. I spent the entire time on the phone. First to Nick, then to my sister. They wanted to know how my first day went. It was, after all, the reason I moved here, so their interest was warranted and genuine. And it was good to talk to them.

Nick and I talked about our friends and what was going on, which was much of the same as it always was. "Sounds like life up there agrees with you," he said. There was no resentment or disappointment in his voice; sure, things between us had fizzled out, but we would always be friends.

"It does, so far. I'm loving it. Did I tell you my landlady is a stoner?"

"The old lady?"

"Yep. Baked as clay."

We laughed and chatted for a bit, and when my phone beeped with an incoming call, I thought it might be Dane, so I said goodbye to Nick and took the call.

Only to find it was my sister. And talking to her was good too, once I'd gotten over the disappointment of it not being Dane. I asked her how the kids were going and she sighed and launched into a monologue to rival a one-man play.

When Wicket was bored with the park and we'd walked far enough, I said goodbye to my sister and went home.

I cooked dinner. No phone call from Dane.

I ate dinner. No phone call.

I let Wicket out to do his business. No phone call.

So I made sure my uniform was ready for the next day and grabbed a quick shower, only to get out and realise I had one missed call.

Of course there bloody was.

It was Dane's number and so I quickly towelled off and changed into my usual sleeping attire of boxers and a T-shirt and hit redial.

"Hello?" he answered.

"Oh, hi. Sorry I missed your call. I was in the shower."

A beat of silence. "Thanks for the visual."

I blushed, thankful he couldn't see. "You know it's Murphy's Law, right? You wait and wait to take a shower and nothing, so finally you think 'bugger it' and take the shower, and of course, that's when you call."

He chuckled. "Yeah. I dunno who Murphy was or what he did to piss off the universe, but he has a lot to answer for."

"He totally does."

"How was your first day?"

"Really good." I was going to leave it at that but figured if he and I had any chance of progressing, then I should be honest. "I think my boss likes me. She's a bit of a hard-arse, but I like her. She takes no crap and I'd take brutal honesty over nice but two-faced any day."

"So would I."

"And the others all seem pretty cool. I think I've got a few of them pegged already. Which ones I'll get along with and which ones I'll have to tolerate."

He snorted. "Oh yeah. The joys of working in a team."

"I actually like it, but I think I've trodden on a few toes. There's one guy, his name's Brian. He's probably fifty-something, and I think he's worked there forever, but I have the sneaking suspicion that maybe he applied for my job and they chose me over him. He seems kinda put out by my being there and was a little bit snippy."

"What did he say to you?"

"The usual 'try and make me look bad in front of the boss' kinda thing. He asked me what kind of management he could expect from me, while my boss was right there."

"What did you say?"

"I told him I'd been profiled under 'situational leadership.' I prefer *democratic*, although I was *laissez-faire* by nature because I like to think my staff responsible enough that they could be left alone to do their jobs without being babysat. I didn't expect anyone to do anything I wouldn't do myself, but if they took advantage and were insubordinate or lazy, I could be a whole lot of *autocratic*. I told him if people did their jobs, we'd get along great. If they were to waste company time and money, they could finish up today."

He gasped. "You didn't!"

"I totally did. And Brian's face was priceless. Like he'd smelt something really bad." I laughed as I remembered his puckered pout. "But you know what? I think Brian and I will get along just fine. Now he knows that, yes, I might be young, but I'm good at what I do."

"Sure sounds like it."

"I had a good teacher. The best, actually."

"Me too. I had a store manager who took staffing seriously, and it really made a difference to where I ended up."

Dane talked about his first job and his horror boss, and I sat on the sofa with my feet up, Wicket at my thigh, stroking his fur. Then he told me how he started with Telstra and how he ended up being the store manager. It was a big job and one he wasn't sure he could handle when he first started, but he had a good team around him and they made it pretty seamless.

I could listen to him talk all night long.

We somehow ended up talking about where we'd lived and the good and bad places we'd rented, where we went to school, our first jobs, and laughed at our childhood crushes.

Apparently, me falling in love with Jimmy Neutron was funny.

"Shut up!" I cried. "I like smart guys."

"He was animated!"

I snorted. "That's just a technicality." He laughed some more. "Okay then, who was yours?"

He didn't hesitate. "Joe Jonas."

"A Jonas brother?"

"Just one. Though I will admit to teenage dreams of more than one brother starring in my fantasy. But that was just once and I can't be held responsible for what my subconscious-self dreamt up when I was fifteen."

I laughed long and loud. But something struck me, a random memory from years ago—a drunk guy at a nightclub thought I looked like Joe Jonas. "So, you like guys with dark hair, dark eyes?"

His chuckle became a hum. "Well, I can't deny it. Yes."

"It just so happens that I have dark hair and dark eyes."

"I saw that," he said, sounding amused. "From your photo."

I wasn't sure what to say to that. He clearly liked what he saw. "I don't always have the windswept, sun-kissed, holding-a-puppy look," I said, aiming for funny to defuse the awkwardness, or tension, or anticipation, or whatever the hell it was that made my heart clench. "Sometimes it's suit pants, a business shirt, tie, and vest. Like today. Even my landlady did a double take."

It sounded like he ran his hand over his face. Did he like how that sounded too? "Is that your work uniform?"

"Yeah. It's pretty smart, but it's not cargos and a faded T-shirt, that's for sure."

"Sounds all right to me."

Oh yeah. I think he liked how that sounded too. There was nothing down the line except for the sound of our breaths. Okay, so it definitely wasn't awkward. Which left tension and anticipation... My belly was full of butterflies.

"Well," he said, "I better let you go. Have a good second day at work tomorrow."

"Okay, yeah. You too... Well, I hope your course isn't too boring." Then I remembered. "Oh, I took some photos of Wicket at the park this afternoon. Want me to send them?"

"Yes, please. If that's okay."

"Sure it is."

"Okay then." He paused, waiting for me to reply.

"Okay then."

"Goodnight."

"Night."

I hit End Call and let the grin spread across my face. I let out a deep breath and a laugh, the excitement of new possibilities too big to hold in.

I sent the photos of Wicket sniffing and rolling in the grass like I said I would. I left Wicket asleep on the couch, got ready for bed, and slid between the sheets. I didn't dream of any Jonas brother, but Stephen Amell made a cameo appearance. His cute little dog was lost but I found him, and he asked me to look after him. I said I would. "What's his name?" dream-me asked. He laughed a warm breathy sound that made me shiver, his eyes shone, and he slipped his hand into mine.

But then Jimmy Neutron turned up and licked my face.

———

I WOKE with a start and found that Jimmy Neutron wasn't licking my face, Wicket was. Then I noticed it was daylight outside and I sat bolt upright in bed and grabbed my phone. Shit. I'd forgotten to set my alarm!

Realising it was only ten past seven and I hadn't missed

work, I could finally breathe. "Need to go outside?" I asked Wicket.

He grinned and jumped off my bed, already heading toward the door.

That was all I needed. To be late on my second day after my spiel yesterday about leadership. Jeez. Wicket had saved my arse.

I watched from the top of the stairs as he did his business, and like he could read my mind, he scooted back up toward me when I thought about having toast for breakfast.

Work was great, and Neda left me alone longer, letting me find my feet. The day flew by, and I thought I even impressed Brian a little. He was probably expecting me to not have a clue what I was doing, having lied on my CV—because there was just no way a twenty-four-year-old could be a manager—but after a particularly prickly customer had spoken to Brian like he was a peasant and demanded free parking, I'd stood beside him and defended him and company policy. With a professional smile on my face and in a matter-of-fact tone, I set the woman straight but let him finish the transaction, all while staring at the now-tight-lipped woman with a smile.

He handed her the room key, and she took her bags and ego and left.

"Thanks," he said quietly.

"Anytime. Everything you did was right, but people will always try to get something for nothing. I don't blame them for asking, but when the answer is no, I expect that to be the end of it." I gave him a smile. "And if someone insists on something outside of policy, come get me. I'll stand by what you tell them."

He gave a small nod, and I took it as a victory. By the time I got home, I was still in a good mood. I took Wicket for a run on the beach, and when I got back, Bernice and K were sitting at the patio table enjoying the last of the afternoon sun.

"Hey," I said, falling into a seat next to K.

"Hey, to you," he said. "Beer?"

"Nah, I'm good, thanks." I held up my water bottle. Then I looked at Bernice. "Thanks again for dog-sitting."

She waved me off. "He's a joy. Truth be told, I'll miss seeing his little hairy face."

K gave his beard a scratch. "Uh, hello? What about this hairy face."

Bernice rolled her eyes and smiled, and for a moment, we watched Wicket sniff in the garden, then go plonk himself down on the grass. "Yeah, I'll miss him too," I admitted.

"When is he getting picked up?" Bernice asked.

"Tomorrow, after work."

"Ah," she nodded slowly. "You're meeting the owner... the cute owner."

I tried not to smile and failed. "I am."

Bernice smiled knowingly at me. "Oh, we're having chicken kebabs on the BBQ for dinner. Wanna join us?"

"You know what?" I replied. "That sounds great. I have some rice salad in the fridge. I can bring it down?"

"Even better," K said.

"Be a doll and turn the BBQ on," Bernice said to K. She nodded toward the old BBQ and said, "She's a bit like me. Old, she don't work as well as she used to, and she takes a bit of get-going to warm up, but once she's cookin'..."

"She's a cracker," K finished for her. The way he looked at her made me glance away, like I was intruding on a private moment. They were an odd couple. They didn't live together; K came and went on his old Harley, but he was here three or four evenings a week. He clearly adored her, and she him.

I'd love to know what happened to her arm and what the scars from her neck to her bicep were from, but it was none of my business. But I could ask her about her tattoos. When we'd had dinner, I quickly stood and collected the plates. "I'll just take these inside."

"Leave them on the sink," Bernice called out. "I'll take care of them."

I'd never been inside Bernice's house before. Sure, I'd seen in through the glass sliding door but never paid it much attention. It was summery, tones of blue, white, and traces of yellow. It felt peaceful. The kitchen was to the left of the door, so I slid the plates into the sink as requested, then went and collected the trays and BBQ tongs as well. As I was walking back out, I noticed a surfboard on a stand in the corner of her living room and huge landscape photographs of the ocean hung on her walls.

She seemed like a free-spirit, so when I sat back down, I nodded toward her full sleeve of now-aged tattoos. "I bet there's some stories in that ink."

Bernice smiled and did that slow nod thing she quite often did. "A lot of stories." And for a moment, I thought that was all she was going to say. Then she took a deep breath and sighed loudly. Not in a resigned way, but more of a wistful sound. "I had a misspent youth."

"Well-spent," K corrected. He grinned proudly. "She was as wild as the ocean. Still is."

She shrugged. "Well, the mind is, but the body can't quite keep up."

"You've lived an interesting life," I said. Not that I knew, but I could sure guess.

Bernice smirked, then pointed to certain tattoos on her

arm. I couldn't discern between the different markings. They'd kind of bled into each other with the help of gravity and time. "Got this one in Phuket. This one in Oaxaca. This one in Malibu."

I was stunned. "Wow."

Her smile was edged with a little pride and a little sadness. "I've been blessed."

She never mentioned the scars, but they felt like an elephant in the room to me. I did my best to ignore it and was saved by the beeping of my phone.

It was Dane. *Can you talk?*

That was odd. I replied, *Sure.*

"Uh, I'm about to get a phone call," I said, standing up. "Thank you, both, so much for dinner and the lovely company. Next time, I'll wash up afterwards."

"Deal," Bernice said. "We might play a bit of music later. We'll try to keep it down."

"No problem. I like the 70s classics. Kate Bush, Fleetwood Mac, Led Zeppelin, Cold Chisel."

"Cold Chisel was the 80s," K said.

"*Breakfast at Sweethearts* came out in 1979," I corrected him. He grinned at me, and I realised it was a test. I was just about to have a dig at him, but my phone rang. It was Dane. I waved them goodnight, called Wicket to come with me up the stairs, and answered my phone. "Hey. Everything okay?"

"Uh, not really."

My heart sank, and any excitement I'd had about where things might have been heading between us sank with it.

CHAPTER SIX

DANE

THERE WAS JUST silence on his end of the line. "Griffin?"

"Yeah, I'm here. What's wrong?"

"Nothing, really. I just woke up today certain it was Friday, thinking I'd see you tonight, only to be bitterly disappointed it's only Thursday."

More silence. Then, "Oh. You asked if I could talk like you were gonna give me bad news."

I snorted. "No. I asked if you could talk so I wasn't interrupting." But then I realised my poor attempt at humour had made him worry. "Sorry. It's nothing bad. Just that I was all excited about coming home but realised I had to wait another day." He chuckled and I breathed an internal sigh of relief. "Didn't interrupt anything, did I?" I asked.

"No, I was just having dinner with my landlady and her boyfriend."

"You've mentioned her a bit," I said.

"I like her. She's... interesting."

That was odd. "Interesting, how?"

"Kinda like the grandma you always wished you had."

Grandma? Then I heard music start to play and he chuckled again. I couldn't hear it well, but the intro was familiar. It sounded like Cold Chisel. "Something funny about *Breakfast at Sweethearts*?"

He barked out a laugh. "No, not at all."

"Won't your landlady get pissed if you play music at night?"

"Uh, that is my landlady's music you can hear."

Now it was me who laughed. "Doesn't it piss you off?"

"Nope. It's not that loud, and it's not too late. I don't have the TV on anyway, so it's like background music. Anyway, I put in a request for this. And maybe some Kate Bush."

"Eclectic requests."

"Eclectic tastes."

My laugh sounded happy. *I* sounded happy. "Hey," I said. "It's Thursday. Aren't you supposed to be watching *Arrow*? Getting your Stephen Amell fix?"

"I am getting my fix," he replied. "I'm talking to him instead."

I rolled my eyes, which he obviously couldn't see. "Very funny."

"Aren't you supposed to be watching *The Walking Dead*?"

"I'm multi-tasking. Watching TV and talking to you at the same time."

I heard him talking to someone else, and I wondered if he had company. I mean, clearly he had company, but I wondered what kind of company he had... Then he said, "Wicket's here on my lap. I told him I was talking to you, so say something so he can hear your voice. I'll put you on speakerphone."

Oh, he was talking to Wicket. The relief I felt was insane...

"Okay, you're on speaker, so talk to him."

God, okay... "Hey, little buddy. I miss you like crazy, but I'll be home tomorrow. You wanna go home? I promise lots of walks and trips to the beach because Griffin tells me you love it."

"He's staring at the phone," Griffin said. "He's listening."

So, I babbled like an idiot for a full five minutes. I told Wicket how Grandma was really worried and how she went walking all the streets to find him. I asked him how on earth he got to Coolum, and if he hitched a ride, what were the people like? I told him I was glad Griffin found him, and how their adventures together made me happy and a little bit sad that I was missing out on all their fun.

I had to wonder who exactly I was telling this to. Wicket? Or Griffin?

After a beat of silence, Griffin said, "Ah, he's uh, he's gone back to his bowl."

"Sounds about right."

"He was listening though. He could really tell it was you."

I didn't know if that made me feel better or worse. "Thanks."

"How was your last day at the course?"

"It was okay. We had a celebratory dinner but it's always an early night because people have to leave the next morning."

"Was it fun though?"

"Yeah, it's always good value. I only see these people once or twice a year, so it's nice to catch up with them."

"Sounds fun."

"The course itself isn't too bad. You know, team-building, productivity, reporting, how to more efficiently manage time and people. Blah, blah, blah."

"Sounds like HR's wet-dream."

I snorted. "I'm sure it is. Somewhere, in some HR office in some far-off city, someone plans this shit and gets off on it."

He laughed. "Thanks. Not quite the visual I wanted to go to bed with."

And now I had the visual of him going to bed. "Sorry."

"Doesn't sound like it. Tends to help if you don't sound so cheerful when you say sorry." He was smiling, I could tell in his voice.

"I was just—" God, I almost admitted to having visuals of him going to bed. "I was just not going to say anything because then it would be weird."

He chuckled again. "And we can't have that."

I smiled. "Well, I better finish getting packed and organised. I'm meeting a few of them for breakfast tomorrow, so I suppose I should go to bed."

"I suppose I should too."

"I'm looking forward to tomorrow afternoon," I admitted.

"Me too. Though I have to say, I'm going to miss Wicket. He saved my arse this morning by waking me up. I forgot to set my alarm. Could have been a disastrous second day if I'd slept in."

Now I was thinking about his arse that Wicket saved. Great. "I'm sure he'll miss you too. And yeah, he's a great little alarm clock. When he was a puppy, he'd wake me at two, at four, and at six. Every night."

"He would have been the cutest puppy."

"I'll find some photos and send them."

"Thanks."

"Okay, I better go."

"Can I ask something real quick?"

"Sure."

He let out a breath. "I don't mean this to sound weird. And I am looking forward to meeting you. And I think we get on well over the phone, but..."

"But?"

"But what if we meet and it's... weird. Or what if you meet me and think 'he's not Joe Jonas' and you're disappointed?"

"Or if you think I don't really look like Stephen Amell?"

He snorted. "I won't care, honestly. But you know what I mean? I have this horrible feeling that I've built up this crazy-perfect scenario and nothing in reality will match up. Does that sound... crazy?"

"No, I get it." And I did. I had him pegged as Mr Perfect, and in reality, that wasn't likely at all. Had my expectations skewed my chances with him? "What if we have a code word for failure to launch?"

"Failure to launch?" He snorted. "I've never had *that* problem before."

Now I laughed. "Well, if you had, there are pills for that."

He chuckled, then said, "I like the idea of a code word. If one of us isn't feeling it or if it gets weird and we want to bail, we need a word. All we have to do is say it, and we can both walk away."

"Sounds fair."

"Do you wanna pick the word?"

I looked around the room. "Um... avocado."

"Avocado?"

"It's as random as any word, I guess. And the socks I just threw in my dirty clothes bag have avocados on them."

He chuckled again. "Okay, avocado it is."

"Righteo then. I'll see you tomorrow afternoon. Out the front of the surf club."

"I'll be the one with your dog."

I smiled at that. "I'll be the guy who's looking for a guy with my dog."

"Night, Dane."

"Goodnight, Griffin."

He disconnected the call, so I slid my phone on to the bedside table and stared at the hotel wall. It was comforting to know that he was on the same page as me. We were both nervous, excited, but wary. Cautiously optimistic but wise enough to know better. I switched on the television but couldn't tell you what I watched.

I was too distracted wondering how on earth I was going to get through the next twenty-four hours.

––––––––

THE BREAKFAST MEETING finished on time and a few of the others were keen to stay around, do some sightseeing, catch up some more. But not me. I was itching to get on the road and get home. I spent most of the drive talking to my assistant manager at the store. She had a lot to fill me in on and I was grateful for the heads-up before I turned up tomorrow morning. It was just the usual stuff: staff issues, budgets, sales reports, marketing goals.

But none of it could hold my interest.

I asked her to email me the reports and spreadsheets, telling her that trying to concentrate on percentages and drive at the same time was too distracting. Not technically a lie, but not the whole truth. I was distracted, that much was true, but not for the reasons I could tell her.

My mind was on getting Wicket back, of course. But also on golden sand, clear blue water, and a guy with a killer smile.

By the time I got home, I'd called everybody I had to call: Mum and my brother, then Scott, my friend to ask about maybe a game of basketball sometime. Bluetooth and long-distance driving were productive, at least. And pulling into my drive was the best feeling ever. I walked inside and dumped my bags, only for it to hit me that Wicket was not there. Usually he was in under my feet, doing crazy jumps and excited burnouts. The silence, his absence was unnerving.

Not long now, little buddy.

I checked the time. I had two hours.

Doing all the chores that needed doing, and after a trip to the supermarket, I grabbed a quick shower to freshen up, changed my outfit five times, and finally—finally—made the fifteen-minute drive to Coolum Beach.

God, I was nervous.

I was also a little early.

I sat in my car for a bit knowing Griffin only finished at five. He'd need a good twenty minutes to get home, get changed, grab Wicket, and drive to the surf club. And that was *if* he left work on time.

But the beach looked too inviting. The ocean was an incredible shade of turquoise today. The waves were perfect. Surfers dotted the breakline waiting for the perfect crest to call theirs. The sand was white gold in the afternoon sun, people were walking the mile-long shoreline, some were jogging, kids were splashing in the shallows, dogs were playing fetch.

Why would anyone want to live anywhere else?

Deciding I needed to be closer, I got out of my car and walked over to sit on the sandbank instead. The salt air hit me like a memory, visions of childhood summers and laughter played through my head like a movie. The breeze was warm, a lovely contrast from where I stuck my feet into the cool sand, and I almost forgot what I was waiting for.

Until, out of the corner of my eye, I caught sight of movement. Something was moving fast and coming right at me.

"Wicket!" someone yelled, and I turned at the name just in time to catch Wicket as he launched himself at me.

He knocked me backwards. Luckily I was sitting down, but he jumped and licked and yipped and licked me some more. I sputtered from the kiss he gave me, laughing and trying to right myself. "Hey, little buddy. I missed you too."

"Guess I didn't need to worry about Wicket not recognising you."

Still trying to contain an over-excited Wicket, I looked up then to see a tall, dark-haired, dark-eyed guy with a killer smile.

Griffin.

Jesus, he was even better looking in person.

Holding Wicket in one arm, I scrambled to my feet, brushing myself down with my free hand. I was now covered in sand, thanks to Wicket. And dog slobber. I wiped my face with the back of my hand and then had to wipe my hand on my shorts; my hair was a lost cause. *Goddammit.*

So much for a good first impression.

CHAPTER SEVEN

GRIFFIN

IT WAS as though Wicket knew we were going to find his daddy. I mean, I'd told him a dozen times, but I didn't actually think he understood me. But he stood up on the front seat of my car, pulling at his harness, looking out the window with his biggest grin yet.

The day had dragged painfully toward five o'clock. Even with the still-new-job excitement and learning curve I was on, I'd spent every spare moment mentally going through my wardrobe so I'd know what I'd wear when I met Dane. By the time I finished, I'd envisioned myself in about fifty different possible outfits but decided to go casual but still stylish. The winning outfit was navy cargo shorts and a light blue button-down shirt covered with tiny pineapples that had cost me a small fortune.

I had a belly full of butterflies and, once I'd pulled into the car park at the surf club, had to take a few deep breaths. I did a quick scan of the surf-club balcony that I could see but couldn't see anyone who might be waiting...

Wicket barked, fixated on something outside his window. His little paws on the car door and his tail a frantic metronome. I followed his gaze, wondering if he could spot his owner. There were a lot of people on the beach this afternoon, and I could see some dogs down by the water chasing a ball or a stick. "Yeah, okay, okay," I said, getting out. I went around and opened his door, and he normally sat and waited patiently for me to clip on his leash, but as soon as I undid his harness, he was gone.

He zipped out of the car, darting around me, and jumped over the post and rail fence. Oh no...

"Wicket!" I yelled, shutting the door and racing off after him. "Stop!"

But it was too late. He didn't run down to the other dogs or the water like I'd assumed he would. He ran straight over to a guy who was sitting on the sandbank enjoying the view, and I watched like it happened in slow motion. Wicket ran as fast as he could and launched himself at the poor guy, who was slowly turning around. "Wicket, no!"

Wicket hit him with so much force, the guy fell on his back, trying to hold Wicket back from licking his face. His legs sprawled out and sand bloomed out from his feet. But as he slowly sat back upright, I could see the guy was laughing, and Wicket was wiggling so hard I thought he might hurt himself.

Then I took a closer look at the guy as I walked toward him. Short brown hair, a bit of stubble, blue eyes.

Oh.

It was Dane.

If I had any worries about turning up here today and Wicket not warming to the guy who was supposed to be taking him, they disappeared right then and there. When I was about a metre away, I said, "Guess I didn't need to worry about Wicket not recognising you."

Dane got to his feet, trying to hold a squirming Wicket,

who was still trying to lick his face. He brushed himself down and wiped his face. Wicket had made a mess out of him; sand and slobber, and if he wasn't dishevelled before, he certainly was now.

I'd never seen anyone so handsome.

He held out his hand. "Dane Hughes."

I shook his hand, warm and strong. "Griffin Burke."

His smile, slow spreading, became a grin, and my stomach did some weird somersault. I think the butterflies were planning a mutiny. "Did you think Wicket wouldn't recognise me?"

"No, well, I just dreaded turning up here and Wicket not wanting to go near you. But I needn't have worried."

Dane just kept on grinning and put Wicket down. He dusted his hands off on his shorts but was quick to pat his dog again. Wicket did a dance between us, up on his back feet, trying to get closer to his daddy.

"He's missed you," I said.

"Probably not as much as I missed him."

He kept bending over to pat Wicket, so I said, "Wanna sit here till he's sure you're really here?"

Dane hadn't stopped smiling yet. "Yeah."

He parked his arse where he had before, and Wicket was quick to jump back in his lap. The sandbank was a bit of a rise, so it gave a great view. I sat beside him, putting maybe two feet between us. "He spotted you from the car," I explained. "He barked, and he doesn't bark very often. At first, I thought he was looking at the dogs, but he ran straight to you."

Dane gave him a bit of a squeeze. "You went off on some great adventure while me and Grandma feared the worst."

Wicket jumped off his lap and onto mine, then jumped

off me and stood between us, looking at us with his tongue hanging out. "I think he's trying to tell me he found you," I said, ruffling the fur on Wicket's head. "You found your daddy, huh?"

Wicket bounced, and Dane laughed. "That's a yes."

Then Wicket climbed back onto Dane's lap and plonked himself down. Like all the excitement was over and he didn't want Dane to leave him again. "Yeah, I don't think he'll be leaving your side anytime real soon."

Dane looked at me. "Thank you. For finding him, for looking after him. And..." He made a face. "And for treating him like I do." He stroked Wicket's fur for a quiet moment. "I'd hate to think what could have happened if anyone else found him."

I took out my phone and scrolled through the photos. Admittedly, I'd taken a lot of photos of him, but I got to the very first and handed my phone to Dane. "That's what he looked like when I found him."

The picture was of a very different looking dog. Muddy, wet, straggly and clumpy fur. It didn't even look like him. "I didn't think it was the same dog I'd seen the day before."

Dane frowned and his eyes went wide. "Is that him?"

I nodded. "The first day I found him, I just thought someone who was hiking owned him. It was hot, so maybe they left him by their car in the shade. He was friendly, had a collar. I didn't look too hard, to be honest. I gave him some water, though. Then the next day I went back to hike again and it had rained, so there was a lot of mud. He was under one of the tables near the public toilets. I didn't think it was the same dog. I got out to see if he was okay and he jumped in my car."

Finally Dane smiled. "That'd be right."

"He sat himself in the passenger seat, and that's when I saw your number on his tag."

"Thank God you did."

"So I took him home, gave him a bath, and who knew there was white fur under that mess?" I reached over and gave Wicket a pat.

"I'll never be able to repay you," Dane said quietly. "I mean, I can give you money for what you spent on dog food or whatever, that's no problem. I just mean, for finding him and taking such good care of him."

"You don't owe me anything. He's been the best thing, really. He got me out and about, having a look around. Being new here, I didn't really know where anything was. Now I can tell you the best parks and best dog-friendly beaches up the coast."

Dane chuckled and then he looked at me for a few seconds. "Well, I still do owe you dinner. That was the original plan, wasn't it?"

Was he asking if he owed me dinner as thanks or if I was still interested in spending more time with him? I smiled. "It was. And yes, I'll let you buy me dinner."

He smiled right back at me, and I noticed a slight dimple on his cheek. "Wanna go for a walk along the water before dinner?" he asked.

"Sure do."

I stood up and Wicket looked up at me, his ears pricked. "Come on," I said to him. "You too."

Wicket scampered off Dane's lap but looked up at him expectantly. "Yeah, I'm coming too."

And the three of us walked down to the water's edge and headed north, up the beach. Wicket chased the ebb, and the flow chased him back, and we laughed at him for a minute as we began to walk.

I tried not to ogle, or at least, I tried not to get caught, but it was hard not to give Dane a once over. He was hot. There was no other way to put it. He was shorter than me by a few inches but much broader in the shoulders. He was athletic looking, thickset, like he probably played league or union at school. Or maybe he still did, I had no clue. There was so much I didn't know.

"So," he started. "You like to hike? And going to the beach?"

"Yeah, love being outside. It clears my head and keeps me fit. I've tried gyms, but weights aren't really my thing and I get bored with treadmills. I like to swim too."

"Oh, I like swimming too," he said. "And hiking. As long as it's not too uphill, I'm good."

"Have you ever climbed Mount Coolum?"

"Once, in high school as part of the sport program, but not since."

"It's good. I'd like to do it again."

He smiled, easy and carefree. "I suppose I could make myself walk it again. A group of buddies and me would meet and play basketball, nothing serious, but it was always good for cardio and a laugh. We haven't done that in a while. I should call them."

I picked up, a little belatedly, that he mentioned school here. "You went to school here?"

"Yep. Maroochydore, born and bred. Mum and Dad moved to Caloundra a few years ago, but I stayed. My brother's at uni in Brisbane."

"Did you go? To uni?"

He shook his head. "Nah. Not really the academic type, but I've done courses since. Went straight into retail out of school, then started with Telstra when I was twenty and went from there. I've done Business Management and that kind of stuff. What about you?"

"Not university, but I've got a hospitality degree. It was subsidised by the hotel I worked for in Brisbane."

"You like working in hotels and resorts?"

"I love it. It's not for everyone, but I'm good at it. Not having weekends off takes some getting used to."

"Tell me about it. I have Mondays and Tuesdays off."

"Me too!"

"Really?"

"Yep, hospitality industry curse."

"Same with retail."

"My ex had normal weekends and mine were Monday and Tuesday, and it wasn't easy."

"Yeah, tell me about it. But that's good that you have the same weekends as me."

"Oh really?"

If he blushed or if it was the setting sun that painted his cheeks, I wasn't sure. He shrugged and changed the subject. "Guess you must be good at it, given you're, what, twenty-four and in management?"

I shrugged. "Not full management. Only second-tier, but good enough."

He gave me a look that told me he liked my modesty. It was half a smile and he squinted one eye against the setting sun.

God, help me. He's not just handsome. He's really cute too.

We walked until the people on the beach were just small dots behind us. Wicket was happy to run ahead, into the water, up onto the dry sand, chasing tiny crabs, and digging random holes until he was bored, then running ahead again.

We somehow ended up playing twenty questions. Favourite movies, bands, songs, colours, books. Though we kept getting sidetracked and talked about a whole bunch of nothing too. By the time we got to the end of the beach, he was telling me a funny horror story of the time he and his mates went to Bali and did what everyone told them not to do. They had eaten at a street food stand and proceeded to spend the rest of their holiday on the toilet. "It wasn't pretty. God, I've never felt so sick. Needless to say, we didn't get any surfing done."

"You surf?"

"Not as often as I'd like. Actually, I haven't for years. You know, work and adulting."

I snorted. "I was thinking of taking lessons," I admitted. "Don't know if I'll be any good at it, but I can't move to the Sunshine Coast and not at least try."

We'd stopped walking and I hadn't even noticed, but the sun was almost gone. The sky was a vivid purplish-pink, and suddenly the crashing waves sounded loud. Or maybe it was my blood in my ears because I realised we were really alone.

"How about we head back?" he said, turning to walk back the way we came.

"Yeah, okay."

Wicket now stayed at our feet, probably tired after running in every direction for the entire walk. I wasn't sure if I imagined Dane walking a little closer to me or if it was wishful thinking. "I can teach you," Dane said.

"Huh? Teach me what?"

"To surf?"

Oh. I almost laughed. "Oh. Yeah, that'd be great."

"What did you think I meant?"

I snorted out a laugh and gave him a side look. "I wasn't sure."

He laughed at that. "I can't promise I'll be a good teacher."

"I can't promise I'll be a good student. Actually, there's a very good chance I won't even be able to stand up on a board. I have an old boogie board but it's not much good for anything. Wicket can stand on it though. Thought it was great fun."

I decided halfway back to the clubhouse that Dane's smile was even better against the sunset.

I must have been staring at him for too long. He shot me an amused but puzzled look. "What?"

"Oh nothing. Just that your photo didn't really do you justice."

His eyes widened, like he couldn't believe I'd just said that out loud. Again, I couldn't tell if he blushed or if the pink sky made his cheeks look like that... "Well, I could say the same for you." He shrugged. "Except you're taller than I thought."

"How tall did you think I was?"

"I don't know. Your photo didn't have height markers."

"Neither did yours."

"I thought maybe six foot. How tall are you?"

"My driver's licence says six one."

"Mine says five eleven, but I think they gave me half an inch."

I chuckled, then realised Wicket wasn't walking with us. I stopped and turned. "Wicket!"

Dane froze, then searched. "Wicket!"

A little white blur came running toward us from up near the brush, smiling, tail wagging. Dane scooped him up.

"No more running off, mister. No more heart attacks. I'm too young to die, and then who would look after you?"

"I would," I volunteered.

"Don't tempt him," Dane said with a smile. "I think he enjoyed his stay with you more than me."

"Nah. I'm like the fun dad who gets the kids on weekends. You're the real dad who has to discipline and make the kids clean their rooms. Not as much fun, but if he skins his knee, you're the one he'll run to."

Dane laughed. "Maybe."

"Maybe? Did you see how excited he was to see you?"

"Yeah, I did." He gave me a smile that felt like a touch. He ruffled Wicket's forehead and put him back down and we watched as he trotted ahead of us. We started walking again and Wicket stayed close this time.

When we got to the surf club, we found a table on the patio where dogs were allowed. "Gimme one sec," I said. "Be right back." I darted to my car and grabbed the bag of the things I'd bought for Wicket and put it on the table. I pulled out the empty water dish and the leash I'd bought for him. "Here. We can fill that in case he's thirsty and the leash in case it's a requirement. Some places are weird about dogs off leashes."

Dane looked up at me. "Did you really buy all this stuff for him?"

"Well, yeah. Of course I did..." I looked down at the other things still in the bag. "I didn't have anything for a dog, so I had to get some things. It's just from the supermarket, nothing fancy."

Dane stood up, and I wondered for a brief moment if I'd crossed some line. I mean, did he want me to feed Wicket off a dinner plate? "I can't believe you paid for all this," he said softly. Then he took out his wallet. "Let me give you some money—"

I put my hand on his, stopping him. "No, it's fine. Like I said, it was my pleasure."

He stared at me and I stared right back. "Then I'm definitely paying for dinner, and I owe you all the surfing lessons you want."

I smiled, then we both realised at the same time I still had my hand on his. Neither one of us moved for a long second, and my heart felt far too big for my chest. He swallowed visibly. "I'll go fill the water bowl," he whispered.

"Okay." I think I managed to nod. I was surprised I managed that. There was definitely some kind of chemistry between us. I couldn't have imagined that just now. Wicket's whining caught my attention. He was near my feet, his ears up as he watched Dane walk away, and he did a little uncertainty dance like he was getting ready to run after him.

"Hey," I said gently, putting my hand on him. "He's not going far."

Wicket looked up at me, so I sat down at the table and picked him up. His little heart was hammering, and he strained his neck to see his owner. Dane soon came back carrying a full bowl of water. "See, here he is."

Wicket started to wiggle again, and Dane put the bowl by the table and gave him a pat. "Did he think I was leaving him again?"

"I think so."

He took his dog, gave him a bit of a cuddle, then put him down so he could have a drink. He clipped the leash onto Wicket's collar and slid the handle around his seat. Wicket seemed to realise Dane wasn't going anywhere without him, and he settled by his feet and was soon sound asleep.

We'd barely had time to look at the menu when a waitress came out to take our order, but Dane ordered the fish and I settled on the veggie nachos. The waitress wrote it down but then looked at me. "Would you like any sides? Beans? Sour cream?"

"No thanks."

"Avocado?"

Did I want to pull the safe word? Avocado was the word one of us had to say to walk away. I looked at Dane and he looked at me, both of us smiled slowly. "No thanks," I said, trying not to grin. "Definitely no avocado."

The waitress left us and Dane looked out across the ocean. It was dark now, though the moon was out, and the sound of the waves and some people laughing on the beach was the perfect distraction. When he turned back to face me, he chewed on his bottom lip. "For what it's worth, I'm glad you turned down the avocado."

"Well," I said, trying to ignore the way my heart was trying to claw its way out of my throat. "You might want to wait until your first surfing lesson before you call avocado."

He chuckled. "We'll see."

Our food and drinks arrived and while we ate, I told Dane about how my third day went at my new job.

"You seem to be settling in okay," he said. "Don't miss home too much?"

"Not really. Not yet, anyway. I mean, I moved out of home when I was eighteen, and a once-a-week phone call to my mum doesn't make much difference if I'm ten minutes down the road or two hours."

"Friends?" Then he chewed on his bottom lip some more. "Boyfriends?"

I sipped my Coke. "Friends, yes. Boyfriends, no. Ex-boyfriend, yes. But no current or even all that recent."

Dane let out a breath and grinned for just a second before he cleared his throat. "I'm not either," he said. "Um, seeing anyone, that is. Not for a while."

"Well, that's good to know. I mean, I'm sure if you did have a boyfriend, he'd be a nice guy and all, but I don't share particularly well."

He smirked. "No?"

I chuckled. "Well, popcorn at the movies, yes. Fries, maybe. Guys, no."

He sipped his drink. "Duly noted. Fries are a maybe."

"Fries *are* a maybe."

"Now, I don't mind sharing my fries, and I'll even share my Pringles on a good day. But I um, I don't share my boyfriend. If I had one, that is. Not with anyone."

"Not even if Joe Jonas offered?"

Dane laughed. "Not even then."

We talked long after the waitress collected our plates, and after she'd asked us, twice, if we wanted anything else to drink, we knew it was time to leave.

Dane collected Wicket's leash. "Come on, little buddy, let's get you home."

I took the bag and dumped the water from the bowl into the garden, and together we walked to the car park. I slipped the bowl into the bag and handed it to Dane, then nodded to my car. "This is me."

Dane slowed his walk until he came to a stop, Wicket looked up at me. "Well, then," he stalled. "Thanks again, for everything." He rocked on his heels. "I guess that's it then. Um, that is, unless you want to meet again?"

"I would."

His smile was immediate. "Okay then. Sounds good."

The incredible buzz of anticipation sent the butterflies in my stomach into a flurry. "Okay then." I pressed the unlock button on my car key, and Dane started to walk to his car, but then Wicket whined and refused to take another step. He pulled back toward me.

It made my heart hurt.

Dane frowned but scooped Wicket up into his arm and walked him back to me. "He wants to say goodbye."

I patted Wicket's head. "See ya, little fella. Thanks for keeping me company on my first week here." Wicket wiggled and panted, his tongue hung out the side of his mouth. "I'll miss you too."

Without turning around, Dane took a step backwards, but Wicket whined again. Dane stepped closer again and Wicket was quiet. "I think he likes it when we're close."

My heartrate broke staccato. "I think so too."

He was standing far too close that any passers-by might think us just friends. The car park was dark, not that anyone was paying us any attention. All I could hear was the sound of the waves crashing and far-off laughter. And the sound of my thumping heart.

I put my hand to Wicket's little face but couldn't take my eyes off Dane's. He watched my mouth, then licked his lips. He murmured, "How close do you think he wants us?"

Still with a hand on Wicket, I slid my other hand along Dane's jaw, gauging his reaction, waiting for hesitation, rejection. I was going to kiss him. He knew it, and I knew it. His eyes met mine and they were dark, inviting.

"Closer," I whispered. Whether I was answering his question or urging myself on, I wasn't sure.

Then I leaned down and pressed my lips to his. Soft and warm, and slow at first, I kissed him. And, like he savoured the moment, he hummed and let me lead until I pulled his bottom lip between mine. Then he lifted his free hand to my neck and deepened the kiss.

Our tongues touched and sparks exploded in my blood. He tasted sweet, his mouth warm and soft, his stubble rough. The contrast made my knees weak.

Then Wicket whined again and we broke apart.

"Did we squash him?" I ruffled his fur. "Sorry."

"Oh, he's fine," Dane said. "I think he's just excited."

He's not the only one.

"Well, I should probably go," I said, letting out a nervous breath. I gave Wicket another pat. "If that's okay with you."

He wiggled in Dane's arm. "I think he's happier."

"Me too."

"Me too." Dane grinned. "I'll send you a photo when I get home. Of Wicket. So you can see that he's happy."

"Sounds good."

We both stood there, neither of us making a move to actually leave. Dane took a step back with a grin. "I'm going now."

"Yeah, me too. Bye." I made myself open my car door, and after smiling at Dane some more, I had to make myself get in. My lips were still tingling from our kiss, my heart was still hammering, and the butterflies were gone, replaced by something much, much more pleasant.

CHAPTER EIGHT

DANE

I BUCKLED Wicket into his harness and smiled all the way home. Okay, it was possibly a cheek-hurting grin, but wow... Griffin was kinda great. And the kiss? Well, that was kinda perfect.

I liked that he was taller than me, and I liked his long, lean fingers when he put them to my face. His touch, his lips, his taste... oh, yeah. Perfect.

I looked at Wicket sitting on the passenger seat. "Yeah, you knew exactly what you were doing when you found him, didn't you?"

He panted happily, his tongue curling at the tip. *Yep, he knew.*

When I got him home, he trotted through the house, sniffing everything to make sure nothing was out of place. I gave him some kibble, and two minutes later he was sprawled on his bed in the living room, legs in the air, sound asleep.

I took a photo and sent it to my mum and brother, with the caption, *Home, sweet home* so they'd know all was well.

Then I sent the same photo to Griffin. *I think someone's tired.*

Looks like someone missed his bed ;)

He planted himself in it, stretched, rolled, and conked.

LOL He's had a big day.

Thank you again so much. For everything. And for tonight. I had a great time.

Me too. Thank you for not being a weirdo.

LOL Same. Though I think Wicket knew exactly what he was doing when he found you.

And the whining until I kissed you... did you teach him that trick?

I laughed at that. *Haha I'm not a dog whisperer. But I'm not complaining. I may have even promised him a treat for doing that though ;)*

Give him one from me too.

I was still smiling. I didn't think I'd stopped yet, but I was suddenly nervous. *Can I see you again?*

Yes.

Relief swooped through me. *When?*

Monday?

Okay. I'm sure I can survive until then.

LOL I'm sure you will. I better go to bed. Thanks for dinner tonight. Can't remember if I said that.

You're welcome. Though I'm sure I owe you more for all you spent on Wicket.

Another lunch or dinner?

Both?

Deal.

Thank God this wasn't a video chat or he'd see the ludicrous grin on my face. *Goodnight Griffin.*

Night. Sleep well.

I wanted to tell him that I'd be going to bed thinking

about that kiss but didn't want to sound like a creeper. But I got ready for bed and pulled back my covers, got in, and man, I'd missed my bed. No matter how nice hotel beds were, there was nothing like your own bed. I sighed, every muscle relaxing into the familiar mattress, and my mind swimming with happy thoughts and, because all roads lead to Rome, went straight back to Griffin and that damn kiss.

I closed my eyes and could imagine the warmth of his body near mine, his hand on my cheek. His lips, his taste, his tongue.

Jesus.

A familiar warmth pooled low in my belly, my balls drew up, and my dick started to fill. Oh, I liked where this was going... I gave myself a squeeze and started to stroke, smearing precome over the head so I slid better in my grip.

Oh fuck, yeah. Just like that.

Then I imagined us back in the car park, Griffin leaning down to kiss me, the way he slid his fingers along my jaw, his lips on mine, his tongue in my mouth.

Then I imagined I wasn't holding Wicket and I could use both my hands. I'd slide my hands around his back and down over his arse, cupping and lifting him so he could wrap those long legs around me. I'd push him against the side of his car, rubbing our cocks together while he kissed me deep, and I'd buck into him, and then he'd throw his head back and groan as he came in his jeans...

My orgasm barrelled through me, my balls tight and my cock throbbing and spilling over my hand. My back arched, legs splayed and I grunted as I shot my load. *Fuuuuuuck, yeah. Just like that.*

It took a moment for my brain to function again, as my body twitched with aftershocks. It was so intense, I had to wonder if I was awake or dreaming. Though the mess on my stomach and chest told me it was very real, and I had to wait for the room to stop spinning and catch my breath before I could get up to clean myself off.

I climbed back into bed, still smiley and spongey, and swirly thoughts of a dark-haired guy who kissed like a god lured me to sleep.

I slept like the dead.

———

I GOT TO WORK EARLY, knowing I'd have a lot to catch up on. Li had everything under control, but there were still reports to fill out, sales data to sign, and rosters to work on. I spent a good part of my day on the store floor helping customers but most of it stuck at my desk. I even stayed back a little longer to get a head start on tomorrow's to-do list, but man, I was glad to get home.

Wicket greeted me with his usual wriggle dance, and after a case of the zoomies, I got changed into shorts and a T-shirt, grabbed his leash, and we set off on our usual walk. "I'm sorry I was gone all day," I told him as we hit the foot-path. "Must be a bit hard after spending all day with Griffin and him taking you on excellent adventures, huh?"

Wicket didn't seem to care. He just kept walking, ears and tail up, happy to be outside now. It kinda sucked knowing that he was cooped up all day though...

My phone rang, and fishing it out of my pocket, I smiled as I saw Griffin's name. "Hey."

"Hey yourself," he said, his voice smooth and happy. "How was your first day back?"

"Hmm, busy."

He paused for a second. "What's up? You don't sound too happy. Want me to call back?"

"No, I'm glad you called actually. I'm just out walking Wicket and I was thinking how much today must have sucked for him after he spent all his days having fun with you."

"I had to work the last two days and he was with Bernice, so it wasn't all me."

"But he still had company." I sighed. "Just feel like a shitty parent, that's all."

He chuckled. "You're hardly a shitty parent. He's like the most spoiled dog ever."

I almost smiled. "Maybe. Still feel pretty lousy though."

"Have you thought about doggy day care?" he suggested. "Even if it's one or two days a week? Or a neighbour who likes him? I'm pretty sure Bernice didn't take him on walks or anything, she just talked to him while she pottered about her yard."

"He has a back yard and a doggy-door so he can get in or out as he pleases," I said lamely.

"Then that's all he needs."

I sighed. "Yeah." His suggestion of a day-sitter sounded pretty good. "I might look into the doggy day care though."

"What if he escapes and runs away again like he did for your mum? He clearly likes being at home because that's where he was trying to get back to, wasn't it?"

"I don't know."

"I think it's safe to assume he was looking for you, or home. He just somehow ended up in Coolum."

"Mmm, maybe." He was trying to mollify me, and he did make me feel a bit better.

"Dane, I'm sure he's more than fine with things just the way they are."

I looked down at him and noted how his tail and chin

were up like he was king of the world. "He's happy now anyway."

"I bet if you set up one of those cameras that monitor what dogs and cats get up to when their owners are at work, you'd see he very happily sleeps all day."

"Yeah, you're probably right."

"And anyway," he continued. "We'll just have to make it up to him on weekends with a hike or a trip to the beach."

"*We* will, huh?"

Silence. "Well, I... Shit, I actually didn't mean to say we. I meant *you* will have to make it up to him with hikes and a trip to the beach."

I chuckled. "No, I think you got it right the first time."

He let out a relieved laugh. "It does sound fun."

"So, is that what we're doing this weekend? Taking Wicket for a hike and a trip to the beach?"

"Sounds good to me. Sounds great, actually. I do have to mow Bernice's lawn on Monday morning though. I should be done by ten."

"Perfect." I smiled. He really did make me feel better. "I'm really glad you called."

"Me too."

———

SUNDAY WAS JUST LIKE any other Sunday, except this one was the day before Monday. The very Monday I was spending with Griffin. So naturally it dragged like a Wednesday, which was my Monday. The store was busy, as usual, and I was covering the second lunch shift and helping an older woman understand her mobile and data usage. When she told me she didn't even know her smartphone could take photos, I knew I was in for a long appointment.

Forty minutes later, dear old Marjorie had a better understanding of her phone and that, yes, using the fun crossword picture does use data, aka the internet. She swore she didn't even know how to use 'that internet the young folk talked about' and she should have never listened to her daughter about getting a new phone. I helped her switch off all the apps that used background data that she would never use, and just as she was leaving, I noticed a guy in grey suit pants. Well, I noticed how he filled the arse of them and how the vest pulled in his waist, his business shirtsleeves rolled to his elbows. From the back view, which was a very nice view, I could see his dark hair was short on the sides, the longer top styled perfectly, coiffed up into some trendy do. I mean, this kind of guy was my ideal wank-fodder, even a casual hook-up.

And I felt immediate guilt for even looking. I mean, things were just starting between Griffin and me, and I was very excited to see where our relationship was headed. I didn't want anyone else; I didn't even want to look at anyone else. It was just that this guy was right in front of me and... incredibly hot.

He was talking to Li and she caught my eye and smiled. "Ah, here he is," she said and waved her hand toward me. The guy she was talking to turned around and grinned right at me.

Griffin.

I looked him up and down, taking in what was clearly his work uniform, and grinned right back at him. "Hello."

His lips twitched. "I had an issue with my phone contract. I was hoping I could speak to the store manager?"

Li started, "I did explain that I could help him, but he was adamant—"

"No, it's fine. I've got this one," I said.

Li gave me a smile that said, *I bet you do*, and left us alone.

"This is unexpected," I said. I couldn't take my eyes off him.

"I'm not intruding, am I?" he asked. "I was passing by, literally walking past, and I wasn't even sure if this was your store."

"The one and only inside the shopping centre." I realised then, that we were standing in the middle of the store, customers and staff milling around us. "Come and sit down." I led him to a station where we would have some privacy. "You're not intruding at all. God, I didn't even recognise you at first."

"Ah, work attire. Not my usual cargos and T-shirt."

I looked him up and down again. "You look great. Your hair..." God, each strand was perfection.

"I actually do my hair for work. Style and product, you know. You've probably only seen it windswept and messy."

"It looks great. Both ways." I shook my head, still not believing he was here in my store and not believing he looked so different, yet the same, and so damn hot. "So, did you really have an issue with your contract?"

He nudged his knee with mine. "No. But I do need to change my address."

"Oh." It was work related and he hadn't come in just to see me. I was a little deflated, I had to admit. "I can fix that right up for you."

I typed on the keyboard and brought up the screen I needed. He quoted his mobile phone number and his details appeared on screen. He leaned in closer to the monitor and said, "Oh, would you look at that. I already changed it. Can you do me a favour and print that for me?" he asked.

It was an odd request but I agreed. "Sure. I'll just grab the printout."

As I went to the front counter and collected the piece of paper, I had to wonder what he was getting at. It was a little strange...

I walked back to him and handed him the printout. He stood up and read the details aloud. "Name, phone number, address." Then he folded it in half, then half again, and handed it back to me. "Dinner at my place, say, seven o'clock?"

I laughed. "Very smooth."

He bit his bottom lip, I assumed so he didn't grin too wide. "I wanted to see you. I did actually have to run an errand at the centre management office, so I wasn't lying."

"I don't mind."

Neither of us spoke for a while, just did that staring-because-he's-so-good-looking thing. "So?" he pressed.

"So, what?"

"Dinner. Tonight?"

"God, yes."

Now he grinned. "Okay. I'll see you then." He touched the folded piece of paper I was still holding. "Don't lose it."

"You could have texted me," I whispered, still smiling.

He licked his lips. "I could have." Jesus, the heat in his eyes made my blood all warm.

I swallowed and let out a slow breath, trying not to give myself away, though I was pretty sure he knew exactly the hold he had on me. He gave a lopsided smirk that almost made my knees give out, turned, and walked out. I stood there for an unblinking moment staring at where he'd just been, and Li appeared beside me. I looked at her. She looked at my ridiculous smile and nudged me with her elbow. "Soooo, who was the hottie who asked for you specifically?"

"That was Griffin."

Her eyes went wide. "The new guy you had dinner with the other night?"

"Yep."

"Jesus," she whispered. "He's the one who found Wicket?"

I nodded. "The one and the same."

"I think I know why Wicket chose him."

I snorted and let my grin just do whatever the hell it wanted. "He asked me to his place for dinner tonight."

Li made an oooooh face. "Please tell me you said yes."

I slid the folded-up paper into my pocket. "Hell, yes I said yes."

She did a little happy-wiggle. "That's my boy. At least one of us is getting lucky."

I barked out a laugh, but then I thought about that... Was I getting lucky with Griffin tonight? Making out? Would we be naked? I could almost feel him pressed against me, his mouth on mine, our cocks aligned, and my balls began to ache.

"Right then," I said, collecting myself and shaking my head clear of those images. "Sales data and projection reports. Sales data and projection reports."

If I said it enough times, my brain might actually focus.

"Yeah, good luck with that," Li said as she went off to greet a customer.

Tell me about it. Now I'd thought about what tonight might bring, I couldn't think of anything else.

CHAPTER NINE

I PROBABLY SHOULDN'T HAVE GONE to Dane's work, but I was walking past and I just happened to look in through the glass walls and saw a familiar face talking to an older lady. I literally stopped, took two steps back, stared some more at how he talked and smiled, and my feet were taking me into the store before I could stop them.

I didn't want to ask for him outright, in case personal visits were frowned upon, but I *could* ask for the store manager... He was just right there, after all. It probably helped that I was wearing my work uniform, so I looked more professional. And when he saw me, it was almost comical. Like some cartoon character, his eyes almost fell out of his head.

Dane Hughes was something special.

And he was due at my place any minute. I'd been home for an hour, cleaned up, optimistically put fresh sheets on my bed, had a shower, and also optimistically paid particular interest to cleaning certain parts of my body.

So maybe douching was more desperate than optimistic, but damn, I wasn't taking a chance. I was pretty sure from the way he'd looked at me earlier that we were on the same page.

Something was going to happen tonight.

At a quarter to seven, I found myself sitting at Bernice's patio table. I kept looking at the side gate, my knee bouncing in anticipation.

"What time did you tell him?" Bernice asked.

"Seven."

She checked her watch. "Give the boy some time, child."

"I know." I refrained from rolling my eyes at myself. Barely.

"What are your plans tonight?"

"I dunno. Dinner somewhere. A walk maybe."

She stared at me for an age and I wondered if she'd had one too many of those brownies she'd made this afternoon. "Or you can order something home delivered and not leave your bedroom."

I barked out a laugh. "Well, I don't know if that's on his agenda."

"I'm sure he won't take much convincing," she said. "I lived with some dear friends of mine in Santa Monica for a few months, back in the 80s, and those two men rarely left their bedroom. Ever. I'm surprised they didn't starve to death."

I smiled at her. "How long were you in the States for?"

"Oh, a while. I've lived all over. Born here, and like a bird, I came back here."

"Where was your favourite?"

"Japan. Such a remarkable place. America was fun, Mexico was... well, I don't remember much of Mexico." She laughed and waved her hand. "Damn tequila." Then she looked out over her yard like her memories could be found there. "Asia is beautiful. Europe's too cold for me. But the Pacific islands really are paradise on earth. You ever been?"

"No," I said with a sigh. "I'd love to travel. One day."

"Do it. While you're young. Go lie on a beach in Tahiti. There's nothing like it. And go do crazy things while you can. You can't be trekking Machu Picchu when you're my age." Then she sighed and sadness crossed her face like a shadow. "I guess it's a different world now though. Everyone's gone crazy."

I nodded my agreement. "Seems like it. I try not to follow the news too much. It's too damn depressing. I'd prefer to go walk the beach or swim in the ocean than watch the six o'clock news."

She lifted her beer. "Cheers to that." She took a drink. "The rubbish those idiot politicians go on with should be a federal offence."

I snorted. "Cheers to that." I didn't have a drink handy, but I would have raised it if I had.

Bernice nodded to the glass sliding door. "Grab yourself a beer."

"Nah, thanks anyway. I might have to drive if we decide to go out for dinner."

"Well, if you got smart, you'd have a few so you couldn't drive and had to stay in. If you know what I mean."

I laughed at that and actually considered it when the side gate rattled, followed by, "Hello? Wicket, come back here."

Then a little, white furry dog bounded on in, tongue lolling and tail wagging. I stood up and took a few steps toward the gate. "Hi! Come in."

Dane took a few uncertain steps into the backyard. "I wasn't sure if this was the right side fence, but Wicket seemed to know where he was going."

I was smiling like a fool, and I held my hand out, which he took. "Come over here. There's someone I want you to meet." I led him around the stairs up to my place and over to the patio table. "Dane, this is Bernice. Bernice is my landlady."

Bernice stood up and held out her hand. Her left arm kind of hung limp, as it was prone to do, and thankfully Dane never missed a beat. He shook her hand and smiled. "Griffin's told me a bit about you. You have good taste in music, by the way."

She smiled, sat back down, and lifted her beer. "This boy here's been nervous as a nun in a brothel. And in case he doesn't tell ya, he'd really rather not go out for dinner but stay indoors—" She winked. "—if you're picking up what I'm putting down."

I closed my eyes slowly and could feel my face go fifty shades of red. "I didn't say that."

"Well, not in so many words," Bernice said with no shame whatsoever. "But if we could say what we meant without the dillydallying, we'd get to the good parts so much quicker."

When I finally looked at Dane, he was grinning at me.

"Well, Bernice. Thanks for not embarrassing me," I deadpanned. "Because you know, I'd hate to be horrified in front of him or anything."

She waved me off like it was no problem, then found Wicket in the garden. "And lookie here, my little gardening buddy." She offered him her hand and he sniffed it, then she patted him warmly. "No more adventures?"

"No more escapes," Dane said. "Thank you for looking after him. Griffin said you babysat him for a day or two."

"It was no problem. He kept me company." Bernice smiled at the dog. "Cute little fella."

"Is K coming over tonight?" I asked her.

She drained her beer. "Well, he wasn't. I didn't put in a booty call, but two beers later and I'm reassessing the situation."

Oh God. That was a visual I didn't really want to have.

"Well," she went on, "you two go on, have yourselves some fun."

"I'll do the lawns in the morning before it gets too hot," I added.

"Not too early, I hope." She gave me a pointed look. "I'd like to think you two might need a sleep-in after tonight." Then she winked.

Oh, sweet Jesus. "Okay then, we'll just be off," I said, pulling Dane's hand and leading him toward the stairs. I called Wicket, who scampered up the stairs first, and no sooner did I pull Dane inside and have the door shut, than I leant against it and buried my face in my hands. "Oh my God. That was so embarrassing."

Dane's laughter made me look up. He was a metre from me, wearing blue dress shorts and a trendy button-down shirt. He looked smart but casual, dressed for a restaurant or a walk along the beach. He grinned at me. "She's a hoot."

I'm sure my face was still beet red. "She is, but damn. She could have let up a bit. I'm really sorry about... well, about everything she said."

He stared at me. "Was she wrong?"

My heart stopped. "Wrong about what?"

"Anything she said," he furthered. "About you being nervous and wanting to stay in tonight?"

Breathe out, Griffin. I exhaled. "Well, I... um..."

Dane ran his hand through his hair. "What happened to the guy who came into my work today?" He raised an eyebrow like it was a challenge.

"Oh." I looked down at myself. "That was my work clothes. This is me when I'm not at work: shorts and a T-shirt."

He bit his bottom lip. "I'm not talking about the clothes. Though your work uniform is hot, I have to admit. I'm talking about the guy who was all sure of himself, handed me his address, and asked me on a date."

"Oh." I tried to swallow and, quite frankly, couldn't. "I guess it's different now you're here and it's just us and my landlady basically told you what I wanted to do. Plus, when I saw you earlier, it was completely spur of the moment. I really was just walking past. Now I've had hours to over-think everything."

He stepped closer. "What have you been thinking about?"

Breathe in, Griffin. I inhaled. "You. Me."

He smirked and stepped closer again. We were almost touching, and by God, I wanted him to touch me. "So you want to stay in?"

I nodded, barely. I actually felt faint. "I keep forgetting to breathe."

He smiled before he licked his bottom lip, then pressed me against the door, and nerves and the need to breathe went out the window. I pulled his face to mine and kissed him, open mouths, tongues entwined, and he wrapped his arms around me and pushed me harder against the door. Then he gripped my arse and grunted, and my knees almost buckled.

A high-pitched bark at our side scared the shit out of us, and we both pulled apart. Wicket was right there, looking up at us, and the look on his little face and the relief of getting that first kiss out of the way made me laugh. "I don't think he liked the noise you made," I said breathily.

Dane's lips were wet and red, kiss-swollen. "Noise? What noise?"

"That grunt sound."

"I didn't grunt."

I nodded slowly. "Oh, yes, you did. It was hot as fuck."

He laughed and put his hand to his forehead. "Well. Now that Wicket's ruined the moment…"

"He didn't ruin it. He just didn't understand what was going on. Maybe if I give him some food, he'll leave us alone for a while." I gave Wicket a handful of diced chicken meat, and he hooked right in so I took Dane's hand and led him to the sofa. I didn't even hesitate; I just pulled him down with me so he was on top of me. I had one leg against the back of the seat and one foot on the floor; Dane fit snugly between my thighs.

"You're not shy now," he said, smiling down at me.

"Now I know we're on the same page."

"We're definitely on the same page," he whispered, and this time when he kissed me, it was slower.

He felt so good against me, on me, like we fit together perfectly. Like all our hills and valleys rolled into one perfect landscape. I could grip his arse like this, and rock our hips together, but he was setting the pace now.

It was tender rocking, deep kisses, spine-tingling, ball-aching, cock-throbbing good.

When it got to the point of taking it further or pulling back, he slowed and kissed down my jaw. "I wasn't expecting this," he whispered.

"What? Making out before dinner?"

He chuckled, and his warm breath on my neck made me shiver. He pulled back and rested his head on his hand. "No. I wasn't expecting this. As in, I wasn't expecting to find you."

"You didn't. Wicket did."

He laughed but his eyes never left mine, and God, it felt like he was looking into my soul. "I never expected to find you."

I put my hand to his face. "We're definitely on the same page."

He kissed me again, but before we could get carried away, he groaned, and breaking the kiss, he put his forehead to mine. "I don't want to stop, but I'm trying to be a gentleman here."

I bit my bottom lip. I could feel his erection, how turned on he was because his rigid length pressed against mine. "I'm all for ungentlemanly things."

Now he growled. "Not helping." He slid back so our dicks weren't aligned but stayed between my thighs. "I don't want to rush this."

He looked kind of pained, so I smoothed out the crease between his eyebrows with my thumb and gave him a smile. "I don't want to rush it either."

He met my gaze, though his was guarded. "Unless you're thinking this is just a temporary thing, a quick fuck even, and it's over."

Now I skimmed the back of my fingers along his jaw. "I was hoping it wouldn't be temporary."

His smile was immediate. "Me either." He pulled away and sat up on the couch, so I swung my feet down to the floor, but he was quick to take my hand. "I was hoping we could maybe see where this goes."

"As in dating?"

"As in, yeah, dating. Or more. If we get on so well and like each other, spend time together, that'd make us..."

"Boyfriends?"

Jesus. I wasn't expecting to have this conversation so soon.

Dane made a face. "I know it's far too early for that..."

"Yeah, it is," I said, squeezing his hand in mine.

"And I don't want to sound desperate. Because I'm not. I just..." He let out an exasperated breath. "I just think this could have potential."

"I get it." I brought his hand to my lips and kissed his knuckles. I did get it. I understood completely. "So, how about we do the dating thing. Officially. And if you can still stand the sight of me in a few weeks, we'll upgrade."

He chuckled. "I'm pretty sure I will."

"I can be kind of annoying," I allowed.

He rolled his eyes. "I'm sure I can be too."

"But I'm happy to give this a shot if you are."

He breathed out a relieved laugh. "Yeah. I am."

I stared at him for a moment. "Just so I'm clear, though, when you said you didn't want to rush this, what kind of time restraints are we talking about? Hours? Days?" Then I squeaked the last word, "Weeks?"

He hummed and checked his watch. "I was thinking until nine o'clock, at least."

"Oh, thank God," I said, pouncing on him and pushing him back on the sofa so I was the one on top this time. He let out a startled sound that made Wicket come running over. I laughed at the little dog. "I'm not hurting him, I promise."

Dane ran his hand over my arse and grinned up at me. "No, you certainly aren't." Then he flexed his hips and I could feel the hardness in his shorts. "Well, in a good way, at least."

I leaned down and kissed him softly. "We'd better shut the door later. If he doesn't like whimpering or groaning or grunting, then we'd definitely better shut the door because I can't be quiet."

Dane's nostrils flared and he swallowed thickly. "Jesus, Griffin."

I kissed him again, teasing his lips with mine. His reaction was swift and perfect; he pulled my face to his in a brutal kiss and slid his hand over the crack of my arse and rubbed, hard. I moaned and he rolled, and together we fell off the couch with a *humph*.

Wicket jumped back and barked, scaring us both. We broke apart with a laugh, but Wicket kept barking until we separated and untangled our legs. "Okay, okay," I said, surrendering. I dragged myself away, got up, and sat back on the other end of the sofa, trying to ignore my hard-on. "I get it. No touching him."

Dane sat, somewhat uncomfortably, on the other end of the sofa. Then he readjusted himself, palming his dick and grimacing. "And here I thought bringing Wicket would be a good idea."

I snorted and Wicket jumped up on the sofa between us and sat there, facing the telly like he was one of the boys. Dane rolled his eyes. "Well, maybe we should eat instead?"

I raised an eyebrow at him.

He clarified. "Food."

I resisted the urge to groan my disappointment. "Food it is, then. What do you feel like? We can order in?"

We settled on Chinese food and watched some house renovation flip show. When the food arrived, Dane insisted Wicket sit away from the couch while we ate there, our legs curled up and leaning on each other a bit, sharing our dinner.

It was fun and sweet, and the closeness kept the sexual tension between us simmering. Something more was definitely going to happen tonight. It was tangible, thrumming with every mouthful of food, every laugh, every touch.

But soon enough, dinner was cleared away and Wicket pawed at the door. "Someone needs a bathroom break," I said. "Come on, we'll go down together."

I opened the door and Wicket scampered downstairs first. Dane and I followed. Wicket was nose down, tail up along the garden bed, looking for an ideal place to pee.

Dane and I waited dutifully. The only light was streaming from my open door. Everything else was pitched in darkness. "Bernice has gone in," Dane whispered.

The curtains at her glass sliding door were pulled across. "Yeah. She must've decided against putting in a booty call to K."

Dane chuckled, then he said, "She reminds me of someone. I don't know who, but she's familiar."

"She's from here," I replied. "But she's lived all over the world."

"She's funny."

"Yeah, but if she offers you any brownies, don't have any if you need to drive, or function at all, for that matter."

His eyes widened. "Really?"

I nodded. "Oh yeah. Her and K, who's as old as her, sit down here and smoke a spliff or share a brownie all the time. Then they look at the world through slits for eyes and everything's hilarious."

Dane laughed, then tried to keep it quiet. "That's funny."

"They're a wild pair, that's for sure."

Wicket did his business, scratched the grass proudly, then trotted back upstairs like he owned the place.

"Right then," I said. "I take it he's done." I started to

walk to the stairs to follow the dog up, but Dane hesitated at the bottom. "Wassup?"

He scratched the back of his head and looked up at me where I stood halfway up the steps. "I um…"

God, did he want to leave?

He licked his lips like his mouth was suddenly dry. "I wasn't sure how tonight was going to go, so I packed a bag but left it in the car, just in case. But I didn't want to assume…"

A slow smile spread across my face. "You can assume. If you want." Hell yes, he was gonna stay the night. "I'll wait here while you grab it."

He grinned and darted off through the side gate, only to reappear a few seconds later with a small black overnight bag in his hand. "Is this okay?" he asked.

I was tempted to say, 'Hell fucking yes,' and my dick twitched in agreement as well. But I settled on, "It's very okay."

I turned and walked upstairs. Dane followed, and when he got through the door, I closed and locked it behind him.

CHAPTER TEN

DANE

I HELD onto my overnight bag, not sure where to put it. I mean, it was only a one-bedroom flat, and if I put it in there, I was assuming that's where we'd end up. Which was where I was hopeful we'd end up, but I didn't want to assume too much. Yes, things were heating up between us, but I'd be happy with hanging out, making out, and me sleeping on the couch.

I'd be a whole lot happier in his bed with him, but like I said, I didn't want to assume.

"Where should I put this?" I asked, holding my bag up.

"In my room," he said, his voice like sex and honey.

Jesus Christ. He wasn't shy. He'd had a few moments of uncertainty, but since we'd admitted we were on the same page, he was well and truly taking the lead.

I liked it. I liked it a lot.

"This way," he murmured, taking my bag as he walked past me. He went down a short hall and opened a door and switched a light on, revealing a decent-sized room with a big bed centred along the far wall. The doona cover was swirls of blue and grey, and it looked soft. Like 'if I laid on top of Griffin in the middle of it, we'd sink right in' kind of soft.

Oh, God. I wanted to try that.

He caught me staring at his bed and smirked. "See something you like?"

"Well, I was just thinking... I bet we'd sink right into that doona."

He put my bag on the floor and pulled his bottom lip between his teeth. "Wanna try it?"

Not trusting my voice, I nodded.

Then he looked around me. "Where's Wicket?"

I stepped out into the hall, looking toward the living room. "He's asleep on the couch." Then I took two steps back into Griffin's bedroom. "Is it okay if he sleeps on the couch? I can tell him to get on the floor if you'd prefer."

He stepped right up close to me and closed the bedroom door. He whispered in my ear, his breath warm, "I don't care where he sleeps. As long as he's not in here with us."

Fuck. His voice, husky and smooth at the same time, made me shiver.

I met his gaze and it took my breath away. "God, Griffin," I murmured before he covered my lips with his. He kissed me with his hands on my face, my neck. He was taller than me, so when he kissed me, he pushed my head back, then he pulled my hips into his.

Fuck.

We stood there for I don't know how long. Time seemed to stop.

I raked my hands over his back, down to his arse, and when I gave him a squeeze, he groaned in my mouth. My cock pulsed and my blood heated, making me gasp for air.

Griffin kissed along my jaw to my ear. "Please tell me you're a top."

I barked out a breathy laugh. "Yes. Fuck, yes." I tilted my head, giving him more neck to devour. And he did.

I was going to come in my shorts if I didn't get us naked. I pulled at his shirt first, lifting it over his head and tossing it somewhere. Then I yanked at the button and fly until they gave in, and I eased his shorts over his arse and let them fall to the floor.

Our kisses became smiling and mouthy, but when I finally got myself undressed down to my briefs, the smile on his face slowly became something else.

Want, and desire, and heat, and demanding.

Oh fuck.

"Get on the bed, Griffin," I said.

His cheeks flushed, but he did what he was told.

"Do you want the lights on or off?" I asked. I didn't mind either way, but I wanted him to be comfortable.

He lay on the bed, palming his dick with one hand, tweaking his nipple with his other, and raked his eyes up and down my body. "On."

Oh God, help me. This was going to be over very fast.

I walked to the bed and put one knee near his foot. "If you keep that up, I'll be finished before we've begun."

He chuckled but groaned when he tweaked his nipple again. His back arched slightly. "Me too. I'm too close already."

I crawled onto the bed and up his long, lean body. I prised his hand off his dick. The ridgeline in his briefs made my mouth water, but I kissed up his stomach instead. Over his chest, up his neck, scraping along his jaw until I found his mouth. I kept my weight off him, but our cocks were so close...

So I rubbed mine against his and he gasped into our kiss. Then I did it again, and he moaned.

He wasn't joking when he said he couldn't stay quiet. Fuck.

He ran his hands through my hair, over my shoulders, down my back, and pulled my hips into his. I writhed and thrust against him, our underpants now sticky with precome, but I didn't care.

I wanted more. I needed more.

"Take out our cocks," I urged him.

He quickly fumbled between us, hands shaking, and he pulled us both free. He didn't need telling what to do next. He aligned us both perfectly and we slid, slick silk on hot steel, and pumped us through his fist.

I smashed my mouth on his, kissing him harder, deeper, and he rolled his hips. Our cocks slid together perfectly, fucking his hand, and then he made a strangled cry, stilled, and shot his load between us.

His cheeks blotched in crimson, his mouth fell open, and his neck corded, and his whole body jerked as he came.

His orgasm beckoned mine and my cock swelled and spilled in his tightening grasp.

"Fuck," he gasped, sucking back a breath. "Oh, holy fuck."

I collapsed on him, boneless and out of breath, and he wrapped his arms tight around me. His knees were spread wide now and he hooked his legs around mine. And for a few perfect, heart-pounding moments, we didn't move.

Slowly, he started tracing patterns on my back. "Did you survive?"

I chuckled. "I think so. Did you?"

"Hell yes." He laughed. "That was the hottest thing ever."

I pulled back and leaned my head on my hand so I could stare at him. "You were the hottest thing ever."

"We're a mess." He didn't look sorry or sad about that. He looked kind of proud.

"We are."

"Shower?"

"Yep." I didn't move.

"Today? Or did you want to wait until we're glued together and we have to shower as conjoined twins?"

I chuckled. "Yes, today."

He waited, and I still made no attempt at moving. He grinned. "Well, the shower won't come to us."

"I know." I sighed. "I just don't know how keen I am to actually get up right now."

He grinned. "Are you ticklish?"

I gasped. "You wouldn't dare!"

Then he laughed. "Nope." Then with a ninja-like manoeuvre, he rolled us over and slowly unstuck our bellies. He leant back on his knees, took his half-limp dick in his hand, and made a show of tucking himself back into his briefs.

Cheeky bastard.

Then with a smirk, he looked down at where my undies were still pulled down. "You have the sexiest dick I think I've ever seen." Then he pouted. "It'd be a shame to hide it in your jocks."

"Then take them off," I suggested.

He grinned like a kid on Christmas morning and whipped my briefs down my legs and off over my feet. He threw them somewhere and made another show of inspecting every inch of my body. "That's much better." He bit his lip and finally met my eyes. "You have a really hot body. I suppose you get told that all the time?"

I shook my head. "Nope."

He made a face that was half-disbelieving, half-crazy.

"Jesus. Your chest has the perfect amount of hair. Your stomach is flat but doesn't look like a hot cross bun, your thighs are... God, I bet you can hold me up against a wall for hours with those thighs." I laughed and he grinned. "And your face." He pretended to fan his. "Don't even get me started on your dick."

I looked at him in his undies, resting back on his haunches on his bed. His long thighs were thin, his hips, his lean torso covered with a spattering of dark hair that ran from his chest down to his navel. He was lean but strong, his jaw could cut glass, his cheekbones were high, his dark hair flopped down into his eyes. His fingers were long and thin, and I would have thought they might be dainty if I didn't know how strong they were.

If there was a checklist of traits I was attracted to, he ticked every single box.

I sat up and took his face between my hands. "You're incredible," I said before pulling him in for a kiss.

He hummed happily, then rolled off the bed. "Shower together or separate?"

I followed him to the door. "How big's your shower?"

"Not huge." He opened the bedroom door and stuck his head out, then quickly pulled back. "He's still asleep," he whispered. Then he snatched up my hand and snuck me across the hall to the bathroom. I glanced to the couch to find Wicket still curled in a little fluffy ball of sleeping cuteness.

Griffin quietly latched the door closed and rewarded me with a huge smile. "See? It's not real big, but I'm thinking that won't be a problem."

He looked down at my dick and it jerked as my mind imagined us being naked and wet, pressed up against each other.

He chuckled. "Didn't think so."

Then he turned around, pulled the glass door open, and turned the shower taps on. It was an older style square shower and it was going to be a tight squeeze…

Then Griffin took his underpants off. His long cock hung, half-hard and uncut, and my dick started to fill again. I had the feeling it was going to be a constant thing around Griffin. He laughed and waggled his eyebrows as he stepped into the shower, wetting first his hair and then scrubbing his hand over his stomach and chest.

God, he looked even better wet.

I stepped in and shut the door. The cold glass on my arse cooled my jets a little, so to speak. But then Griffin shuffled around to let me under the spray. "Your turn."

I let my head fall back and closed my eyes as the water coursed over me. Then, soapy hands were on my stomach and chest, cleaning the mess off me. I brought my head forward, looked up into his eyes, and stood on my toes so I could kiss him. I wobbled a little and he showed some mercy and pushed me against the shower wall. Then, lifting my chin, he kissed me instead. It really was much easier.

I'd been with guys who were taller than me before, and it had never been an issue. More a logistics problem that made getting creative fun. The fact Griffin had no problem in leading or being forthright, demanding even, helped a lot.

Before we could get too carried away, he slowed the kiss and pulled away. "Damn," he whispered.

"Hmmm. Exactly."

He groaned and stepped back as far as he could. "I should get out now," he said, opening the door.

I shut the water off and he handed me a towel. We dried off and I ignored my lengthening dick. Surely it could mind its manners for another hour or two. With our towels tied off around our waists, Griffin opened the door, and sitting there like a parent busting their kids was Wicket.

"Oh," Griffin said, surprised. "Did you hear the shower going?"

Wicket looked up at us like he knew damn well what we'd been doing. I laughed. "Just give us a minute."

I picked up my overnight bag and took out my pyjama boxers and a T-shirt. Griffin wore longer sleep pants but forewent the shirt. I didn't mind, not one bit.

"Are you sure it's okay if I stay?" I asked. It was late, but it wasn't *that* late. If I left now, I could be home by midnight.

He took my wet towel. "Of course it's fine. Stay the whole weekend if you like. We can do something fun tomorrow. Go for a hike or to the beach. Go up to Noosa, even. I don't mind."

"Sounds good." It sounded better than good. It sounded perfect, actually, but I didn't want to act too keen.

"And if you want to go home at some point, that's okay too. No pressure." He shrugged. "I'd prefer you to leave at some point than get sick of me. You just have to say."

I huffed at that because it was utterly ridiculous. "I can't see that happening. But, just so you know, I will have to be home by Tuesday afternoon. You know, laundry, groceries. That kind of thing."

"Ugh, yeah. Me too."

Wicket jumped up on the bed and sniffed around. I laughed. "He's probably trying to figure out why he can smell me on your bed." I scooped him up off the bed and said, "Come on, last pee-break, then it's sleep time for you." I looked at Griffin. "I'll just take him downstairs. Won't be long."

Griffin smiled. "I'll brush my teeth."

I stood on the third step from the bottom and waited for Wicket to do his business, and by the time we were back upstairs, Griffin was done in the bathroom. "Can I get you a drink or anything?" he asked.

"Actually, a water'd be great. I'll just brush my teeth too." Wicket was already back in his favourite spot on Griffin's couch, so I took my time getting my toiletries bag and brushing my teeth. Sure, it was okay if I stayed the night, but we hadn't exactly discussed sleeping arrangements.

I came back out to find the lights off, except for a soft glow in the bedroom. I stood in the doorway just as Griffin was straightening the bedcovers from our earlier romp. A bedside lamp cast a muted light across the room, making his skin look even paler, his hair even darker. I couldn't help but stand and watch for a second, then he reached out and pulled the top cover back. "So? Left side okay?"

Relief, excitement, and something warm and lovely flooded through me. "Very okay."

I slid into bed as he did. He pulled the covers to our waists and we settled down, lying on our sides, facing each other. "I'm really glad you're here," he said softly.

"I'm glad I'm here too."

He leaned back and turned the light off, casting the room into monochrome. Then his warm fingers found mine, and he held my hand as we fell asleep.

CHAPTER ELEVEN

GRIFFIN

WAKING up with someone in my bed felt nice. Waking up and realising it was Dane in my bed felt fucking amazing.

Sunlight framed the pulled curtain, so I grabbed my phone from my bedside to check the time. It was seven thirty. Not wanting to wake Dane, I slipped out of bed and opened the bedroom door as quietly as I could. Wicket met me at the door, sitting there with that same judgey 'what are you doing with my daddy' look to his cute little face that he had the night before.

I stepped into the hall and closed the door behind me. "Come on," I whispered to him. "I'll take you out."

I opened the door and Wicket trotted down the stairs. I walked halfway down and sat on a step, waiting for him to do this thing. He peed and sniffed and wandered for a full five minutes and I spent every second squinting, trying to get used to the blinding sunlight. When I'd had enough, I went back inside, leaving my door open so Wicket could come and go as he pleased.

I had no clue what Dane preferred for breakfast, but I started with coffee and toast, thinking that was a standard for most. When the toast was done, Wicket came scooting back inside. "Oh, I see how it is," I said to him, sneaking him a bit of buttered crust. "You only want me if there's toast involved."

"Amongst other things," a croaky voice said behind me.

I turned to see Dane, all sleep-crumpled and sexy as hell, standing there in his PJs. His hair was a mess, he had scruff, one eye wasn't opening too well, and there was a crease down the side of his cheek. He'd never looked sexier.

"Good morning," I said cheerfully.

"Morning." He swallowed hard and bent over to give Wicket a scratch and nodded toward the open door. "Did you let him out already?"

"Yep."

He scrubbed his hands over his face. "Thanks."

It was pretty clear to see that Dane wasn't a morning person. He was still half asleep. "Here, have some toast." I handed him a slice. "It's just got butter, nothing else. How do you have your coffee?"

"Strong, milk, no sugar." He scrunched up his face, then shook his head, trying to wake up. "Thank you."

I chuckled as I made our coffees. "Does it take you a few minutes to wake up every morning?"

He chewed his mouthful of toast and nodded. "Um, yeah. Sorry."

I handed him a mug of coffee. "This should help."

He took it, sipped it, and sighed. "That's really good. Thank you."

I popped some more bread into the toaster. "You're welcome."

"Are you always so awake first thing?"

"Yep. I wake up ready to go."

He sipped his coffee again and ate more toast, but a smile lurked at his lips. "Is that so?"

I had to think about what I said. "Well, that too. But you were asleep."

"For future reference, you have my full permission to wake me if you need to. I won't mind one bit."

I sipped my coffee. "I'll keep that in mind."

He smiled behind his mug. "Well, I'm awake now. What plans did you have for me today?"

The way he asked was laced with innuendo. I looked down at his pyjama bottoms to find a definite protruding half-hard silhouette of his dick, and it made my belly tighten.

"Breakfast?"

The toast popped up but I ignored it. He smirked. "Uh, your toast?"

I licked my lips. "I wasn't talking about food."

He put his coffee down and I grabbed his hand and led him back to the bedroom. I shut the door to keep the dog out and pushed him back onto the bed. He went willingly, with an 'oh, hell yeah' smile on his face.

I pulled his pyjama bottoms off, making his now-hard cock bounce back and smack his navel.

Oh, hell yeah, indeed.

I crawled over him, and taking his shaft in one hand, I licked his cockhead.

He wasn't smiling now.

"Oh, fuck." His head fell back onto the mattress and his hands went to his hair. "God, Griffin."

I sucked him into my mouth and he moaned, lifting his hips off the bed. He was so into this. I worked him over, enjoying the way my own cock rubbed against my sleep pants. But as soon as I thought about my own dick, I needed to touch it.

I slid my right hand down my pants and started to stroke myself while still working on Dane. I sucked him into my mouth, taking him as deep as I could go, and his filthy groan sent me soaring toward my peak.

I moaned around his dick and he throbbed in my mouth. "Griffin," he cried, his tone a warning that he was too close.

I sucked harder, but I pulled off and knelt back before he shot, jerked my own cock harder, and Dane's groan as he came and the smell of sex sent me over the edge. My cock spilled, shooting streams of come to mix with Dane's on his belly.

"Holy shit," he breathed. "That's so hot."

I fell forward then, utterly spent, and Dane caught me. He was half sitting up and I had my forehead on his shoulder, and thankfully, we didn't smear any mess between us. It took us a moment to catch our breaths, and not capable of doing much else, all I could do was chuckle.

Dane ran his fingers through my hair, pulling my head back so he could plant a kiss on my lips. "I think your toast is probably cold."

I laughed and climbed off him. He was a mess, but I was unscathed. "I'll go make some more. You... probably should shower."

He stared down at his belly, at the mix of our come, and grinned. "I probably should."

I fixed some more toast, made more coffee and had eaten the first two pieces by the time Dane came out, showered and dressed in clean shorts and a slightly crumpled T-shirt, his hair wet and neatly brushed. "Well, you look like a new man," I said.

He grinned and took a piece of toast I held out to him. "Thanks."

"I need to mow Bernice's lawn, then I'll have a shower, then we can head out somewhere," I suggested.

"Sounds great."

I changed into some old shorts and plucked a T-shirt out of the dirty clothes hamper so I could mow the lawn. Dane sat on the steps up to my place while I lifted the roller door and wheeled out the mower. Wicket sniffed in the garden, none too fazed by the sound of the mower, just merely inconvenienced when I mowed a strip of grass he was intent on sniffing.

It really didn't take me long, but when I was almost done, I looked up to find Dane gone. Only to see him now sitting at Bernice's patio table with her, both of them with a glass in their hands while I worked up a sweat mowing the lawn. They laughed at my expression, then laughed even louder when I flipped them both the bird.

When I was done, I emptied the clippings into the green waste bin and hosed the mower down, then planted my arse in a chair next to Dane. There was a glass of what looked like orange juice on the table in front of me, a ring of condensation around the base. It looked cold, and when Bernice nodded toward it and said, "Looking at it won't keep you hydrated," I downed half of it in one go. Yep, it was OJ.

"It's hot already," I said.

Dane gave me a smile. "We can hit the beach if you want?"

I nodded, then finished my juice. "Sounds good. I need to shower and change first though."

"Okay," he said. "I'll stay down here while you go do that."

He and Bernice looked comfortable enough, and the sly smile she gave me told me that Dane was about to receive an inquisition.

"Thanks for the drink," I said, putting my empty glass on the table.

"You're welcome," she said.

I was halfway up the stairs when I heard Dane say, "Oh, Wicket, don't roll in that!" and I'm sure he heard me laugh.

But fifteen minutes later, I was showered and dressed and went back downstairs. Dane and Bernice were still at the patio table, laughing about something, and Wicket had a vivid green smear from his face to his stomach.

"Ah, here he is," Dane said. "I was just telling Bernice how I was going to give you surfing lessons one day."

I sat beside him, our knees brushing. "And I'll give you a lesson in patience and humiliation."

He chuckled. "It's been years since I've been on a board, but I'm sure you're not *that* bad."

I scoffed. "I can barely manage a skateboard."

"It's not quite the same," Bernice said. "Theoretically, your centre of gravity is different." We both stared at her and she shrugged. "I can do both."

"You can ride a skateboard?" I asked. "I mean, I saw the surfboard in your living room and I assumed it was yours, but a skateboard?"

Bernice lifted her chin. "I'll have you know, I skated with the best of them in the late seventies and eighties. Those arseholes at Venice Beach told me girls couldn't do a frontside 180. So I did a 360 hardflip and shut that fucker up."

Dane choked on his drink, and I laughed. I was used to her language, he clearly wasn't.

"Sorry to drop the f-bomb on ya like that," Bernice said,

clapping Dane on the back. "But there's only one sure way of pissing me off, and that's telling me I can't do something." Then she sighed and lifted her left shoulder and let it fall, like a shrug but not, and she looked down at her useless left arm like she resented it for not working like it should. She settled on a frown instead and got to her feet, stacking the empty cups. "If you're serious about the surfing lesson, I can give you some pointers. Another day though. K and I can take you out and show you how it's done."

"Really?" I asked, my smile widening. "That sounds awesome! Thank you! Let us know when you're free."

She waved me off and went inside, the glass door sliding shut behind her. I gave Dane a nudge. "Was that okay?" I asked quietly. "I mean, you can still give me some lessons but it'll be pretty cool to have her and K showing us. They're old, but they're cool."

"Oh yeah, that's fine. It'll be fun." But then he frowned.

"What's up?"

"I can't place where I know her from."

"You should ask her. If she doesn't want to tell you, she'll tell you to eff off."

He snorted. "Yeah, I suppose she would."

"Come on then, let's go find a beach."

He stood up. "This is the Sunshine Coast. It's all beach."

"Well, a beach with a café close by that sells coffee and puppacinos."

He rolled his eyes but he smiled. "Yeah, come on Wicket," he called to his sleeping dog. "We can't forget you too."

Wicket got up, shook himself, and grinned. Ten minutes later, we were in Dane's car heading to Noosa.

———

"I DON'T THINK he likes being in the back," I said, looking around at Wicket in the back seat. Dane had taken the dog harness from the front seat and clipped it into the back. Wicket could put his paws up on the car door and look out the window but didn't seem impressed with the view from the back. "Maybe we could put the window down for him."

Dane laughed. "You spoil him so much, he'll resent coming home with me." He rolled the window down and grinned at me. "Happy now?"

I looked at Wicket's grinning, windswept face. "He's much happier now."

Dane looked just as happy. He held his left hand out toward me, palm up. I wasn't sure what I was supposed to do with it. "Oh," he said, kind of dejected. "If you don't want to hold my hand..."

"Of course I do!" I said, grabbing his hand in mine. "I thought you wanted a high-five or something."

He laughed and we drove the rest of the way in silence, holding hands and smiling. With the windows down, the sea breeze was warm, the sunshine bright, and it was pretty amazing. I could get used to this. Very used to it.

He found a park not far from Hastings Street, we hooked up Wicket's leash, and we started to walk. I did have to wonder how he would act in public. It certainly wasn't anything we'd discussed, and holding hands in the car was one thing, but walking down the street was something else entirely.

But Hastings Street was busy, as per usual, so we were walking single file for a bit anyway. But then Dane ducked into a walkway that led to the main beach and soon we were walking on white sand overlooking the aqua-blue ocean. "Wow, the water is clear today," I mumbled.

He stopped walking and took his thongs off, so I did the same. It was easier to walk on the dry sand barefoot. He carried his thongs in the hand he held the leash with and looked at me. "Um, can I hold your hand?" he asked. He looked up the shoreline. "As we walk. If you want to, that is. I don't mind—"

I slid my hand into his. "Thought you'd never ask."

He grinned and the three of us headed down toward the waterline. And just like that, without a care in the world, the three of us walked, talked, and laughed. No one looked twice at us, no one cared. A few people smiled as they passed us going the opposite way, some even said 'G'day.' We let Wicket off his leash for a bit, and he chased the foam in and ran out again as the wave chased him back. He picked up some driftwood and we played fetch for a bit, and every time one of us threw the stick or ran with him, we'd fall back in beside each other and take each other's hand.

At the far end of the beach, where the tourists didn't go, we found a shady spot and sat down. There were some surfers and the occasional jogger, but we were pretty much alone.

Wicket dug until the sand was damp and cooler and then planted himself and, in two seconds, had his eyes closed.

Dane moved a little bit closer to me so our shoulders touched, and he dug his feet in under the sand too. He sighed contentedly. "This isn't a terrible way to spend a Saturday. Well, it's Monday for those suckers, but it's our Saturday."

I snorted. "Nope." The truth was, I didn't know if the term 'perfect day' had been defined officially, but I reckoned this was close. I lay down with my hands behind my head and closed my eyes. "Not terrible at all."

I felt Dane lie down beside me, then felt him shuffle a little closer. Smiling, I peeked at him to find him on his side, with one arm folded under his head, and he was staring at me.

"You know, you're really beautiful," he whispered.

I snorted. "Are you high?"

He chuckled but didn't look away from my eyes. He licked his lips. "How the hell are you still single?"

Jesus. My heart clanged in my chest, but I stared right back at him. "I'm kind of hoping I'm not…"

He huffed a little laugh and smiled as faint colour tinted his cheeks. "I'm kind of hoping you're not too."

"I thought we discussed the officially dating thing already."

"We did. I just meant, why has no one snapped you up yet?"

"Well, my last boyfriend was my best friend and we spent years leading up to it, but it didn't work out. We're still best friends, actually. His name's Nick, and he's a great guy. We just weren't meant to be together in that way. But I can be pretty bossy and I like perfection. Which is probably why I'm attracted to you."

He rolled his eyes. "Now who's high?"

I rolled so I faced him. "What about you? Because you might not be utterly perfect—" I rolled my eyes. "—but you are kinda wonderful, so why is no one knocking your door down? Or are they, and I just don't know?"

His smile turned a little sad. "I don't know. You'd probably have to ask my exes that. I'm not into bars or clubbing, and I work every weekend too. Actually, I work a lot. I have Wicket."

"They were opposed to a dog?"

"No, they were opposed to me bringing him along everywhere."

I frowned at that. "They sound like arseholes."

He bit his bottom lip. "You don't seem to mind though."

"I don't mind at all. In fact, I love bringing him along. Actually, if I had to choose between you and Wicket, I'm not sure..."

His mouth fell open and I pushed his shoulder and laughed. "I'm kidding. I choose both, or neither. You're a package deal, I get it."

Dane's laugh was deep and rumbly, his eyes crinkled at the sides. "We are a package deal." He leaned in close, our noses almost touching. "I like that you get that. You get me."

I closed the distance and kissed him, sliding my hand from beneath my head across his jaw. He opened my mouth with his and deepened the kiss, pushing me back and half rolling on top of me. God, he was so warm, he tasted so good, and he smelt divine. I almost forgot where we were, that we were in public, and as much as I wanted to pull him on top of me, I refrained.

Wicket barked and made a growly huff noise. Dane ended the kiss slowly, resting his forehead on my cheek, and said, "Goddammit, Wicket. He's not hurting me."

I laughed at the dog. He was sitting there, watching us with his head cocked to one side. "No, but we should definitely keep the bedroom door shut tonight," I said, kissing Dane's ear and letting my lips linger. "Or he'll think you're hurting me."

Dane turned his face, his forehead almost touching mine. His eyes were dark, his nostrils flared. "Griffin, Jesus." Then he palmed himself. "You probably shouldn't say stuff like that to me in public. I don't want to get arrested."

I laughed and kissed his cheek, then jumped up to my feet. "Come on, let's go grab some lunch. I'm starving."

———

THREE HOURS LATER, we'd had lunch and taken a walk through Noosa National Park up to the lookout. It was an easy walk, if a little steep in places, but it was made for tourists straight off Hastings Street. By the time we got back, we'd worked up an appetite for an early dinner, so we grabbed some prawns, two six-packs of beer, and headed back to my place.

Bernice and K were sitting at the back patio when we arrived, so we cracked some beers, shared the prawns, and settled in for the afternoon.

Wicket plopped himself down in the shade and didn't look as if he'd be moving anytime soon. Bernice put on some Kate Bush and Stevie Nicks, and the four of us sat around talking and laughing until the sun called it a day. Dane put his hand on my leg at one point, held my hand, or rubbed my arm, and Bernice and K never batted an eyelid. I really liked them. Despite our age and generational differences, they were incredible people who had worldly perspectives on life and amazing stories to tell. I could listen to them talk all night...

Until Bernice took a squinted puff on her joint. "So, which one of you is the vocal one?"

We stared, and my face went crimson.

"Last night," she furthered. "One of you was doing something right."

"Oh God," I mumbled, wanting to die, but taking a mouthful of beer instead.

But Dane surprised me by laughing. "Well, I can take credit for the doing-something-right part."

K laughed loudly. "Don't be embarrassed," he said, clapping me on the shoulder. "You should hear the noises she can get out of me."

Please, Satan, crack open the earth and swallow me whole.

Bernice snorted and looked at K. "Why do you think I play music loud some nights. So the neighbours don't know you're getting your freak on."

I buried my face in my hands. "This feels like my parents have just started *the birds and the bees* conversation with my boyfriend."

Dane laughed and took my hand, peeling it from my face, and lifted my knuckles to his lips. But then he looked at me for real and stood up. "On that note, we'll be off. Enjoy the rest of your night." He called Wicket.

I stood up, so very grateful, and waved them off. "Night, guys."

K raised his beer bottle. "With a bit of luck, we'll both have some music playing tonight, huh?"

I was too embarrassed to do much more than wave, but as soon as we were inside, I shut the door and leaned against it. "Oh God, that was so embarrassing. Do you think she really heard me last night?"

Dane, trying not to smile too big, came over and lifted my chin. "Don't be embarrassed. The noises you made last night were the hottest thing I've ever heard." I frowned and he kissed me. "And don't censure yourself. I'm hoping the noises I can get out of you tonight will be even better."

Then Wicket barked beside us again. "We're too close for his liking, I think," I said.

"Mmm," Dane said, stepping back just a little. "Well, he

needs to get used to it, because I don't want to stop anytime soon."

The music downstairs got me thinking. "I have an idea. Can you dance?"

His eyes went wide. "That depends..."

I snorted at his expression, and taking his hand, I led him to the space between the kitchen and the living room. I turned to face him. "Slow dance with me."

Dane pulled me close, held one hand up to our chests and slid his other hand around my lower back. We moved our feet and did actually dance as Stevie Nicks sang "Rhiannon" and "The Edge of Seventeen," and Wicket didn't seem to mind. We stayed like that for a few more songs, and Wicket soon lost interest. Though when I started to work my hands over Dane's back, feeling his shoulders, his waist, his arse, his lips found mine, and by the time Kate Bush was singing "This Woman's Work," we weren't dancing anymore. We were standing in my living room, kissing deeply, passionately. And when Kate Bush and Peter Gabriel were telling us not to give up, we were both hard and handsy, moaning and grinding.

Wicket was sound asleep on the couch.

CHAPTER TWELVE

GRIFFIN WAS A PARADOX. So shy about some things, so very forthright about others. When he said he was bossy, he wasn't kidding. We'd had the best day. The beach, a hike through the national park, good food, some beers. We'd held hands, we'd made out. Being with him was so easy. There was an ease between us like we'd known each other for years, but that *this is new* excitement kept my nerves thrumming and my heart thumping.

God, when he was lying on the beach today in the shade with his eyes closed, he took my breath away. Grains of fine sand caught on his eyelashes and the filtered sunlight made him look earthy and warm. He had a spray of freckles on his cheeks, a few strands of his dark hair flopped down on his forehead, his fine-pointed nose and cupid-bow lips... But then he'd looked at me with those brown eyes with flecks of gold and my heart tried to claw its way out of my chest.

Yeah, I was in deep already.

After what? A week? A week of texts and phone calls, one date, and a full twenty-four hours together?

The way he'd blushed and shrunk in his seat when Bernice had embarrassed him made me want to save him. He was mortified and wary when he got upstairs, but then he bravely made me dance, and half an hour later he certainly wasn't being shy.

The whole day had led up to this.

He'd hinted earlier that he'd be making noises as though I was 'hurting' him later, his tone dripping with innuendo, his eyes not even trying to hide what he wanted.

He was wrong about one thing though. I would never hurt him.

There was something unsaid, yet implied, heavy in the air, about where this dancing was taking us. The music was forgotten, we no longer moved our feet or swayed. We stood there, wrapped around each other, mouths joined, hands desperate. Griffin set the pace, and I followed his lead. If he wanted nothing more than this, I'd happily do this all night long. If he wanted to end up in bed with me inside him... Oh, God.

I shivered and moaned, and Griffin broke the kiss. "What?" he asked.

I could hardly tell him just imagining being buried inside him almost made me come. "You're really turning me on," I said.

He gave me a sultry smile. His lips were kiss-swollen, wet, and pink. I wanted to taste him again, but then he put a hand to my face, rested his forehead on mine, and closed his eyes. "I want you to take me to bed," he whispered.

It took me a moment to answer. I kissed him softly. "Okay."

"Dane," he said, his eyes open now. Dark and honest, exposed and vulnerable. "I want you to fuck me."

My blood ran hot and my balls ached and my cock pulsed. All I could do was nod.

He answered with a smile, took my hand, and led me to his room. He closed the door behind us and slowly, like it was a performance just for me, he walked over and switched on the bedside lamp.

He pulled his T-shirt off and gave me a shy smile. Then he met my eyes and slid his shorts and briefs off without looking away. He stood there, naked and beautiful, slowly stroking his long cock.

"Fuck, Griffin." I dry swallowed.

He smiled victoriously and went to his bedside drawer. He took out a bottle of lube and some foil wrappers and threw them on the bed, then climbed on after them. He lay there, legs spread wide, slow-stroking his long cock, while I could barely breathe.

"You're very over-dressed," he murmured. Then he took the lube and poured it onto his hand, never breaking eye contact as he reached down to his hole and slicked himself.

Then he slipped in one fingertip and arched his back.

Fuuuuuuuck.

"Dane," he growled impatiently.

I shot into action, stripping my clothes and kneeling on the bed. I crawled so I was between his legs and leaned over him, looking down at his face. "You are so beautiful," I whispered, then kissed him. Slow at first, then deeper and harder, until his hands went to my face, then my hair.

He was smearing lube all over me and I didn't care. I was so turned on, I could barely think. He rocked his hips up to meet me, desperate for friction, so I pressed down on him, letting him feel my weight.

He hummed low in his throat and lifted his knees to our chests, and I knew then he was getting more than desperate.

Breaking the kiss, I pulled back. "How do you want to come? Before I'm inside you, while I'm inside you, or after?"

His nostrils flared and he gripped his hair like he was struggling to compose himself. "Fuck. Before and during."

Twice? Jesus Christ. I added lube to my fingers and rubbed his arsehole. "And after, if I can coax a third." I slipped a finger into him.

Griffin arched his back and moaned, then he gripped his own dick and started to stroke. "God, Dane, I'm so fucking turned on right now," he whined, rocking his hips and stroking his cock.

I pushed in another finger and he pushed back on my hand, his mouth fell open, and he went rigid as his orgasm ripped through him. He came hard, silently, shooting ropes of come onto his stomach before he slumped back on the mattress.

"Oh, damn," I murmured.

He gasped back a breath then writhed in front of me. "Dane, need you to fuck me now."

Right then. This was where the bossiness came into it. I fumbled with the condom, grimacing as I rolled it down my length. God, this was going to be over way too fast. I gave the base of the head a squeeze to stem the urge to come a little, then spread more lube over my cock and his hole. I pressed the blunt cockhead against his entrance and eased inside him. He gasped and whined, so I leaned over him and kissed him while I breached him.

He lifted his knees higher and I slipped in a bit further, but he was so tight. So fucking tight. I groaned into his mouth and he lifted his hips in response. I squeezed my eyes shut, trying to rein back the overwhelming urge to thrust and fuck. When he held my face, I opened my eyes and found him staring at me, wide-eyed and full of wonder. "Oh my God, Dane, yes."

"You feel too good. I'm not going to last."

"Yes, you will," he said, rolling his hips back and forth so I sunk deeper inside him. "Oh yeah, all the way in." His voice was gruff and he pushed his head back, the veins down his neck protruding.

He was, without doubt, the sexist man I'd ever seen.

I was buried all the way inside him, every inch of me, and he took it, wanted it, wanted more.

He whined until I pulled out a little and he moaned when I slid back in; the most incredible sounds that made my balls ache, longing for release.

But he wasn't ready yet. He said he wanted to come again while I was inside him, and so I leaned back and fisted his still-hard cock.

"Oh fuck!" he cried as I pumped him in time with my cock inside him. "Yes. More. Just like that. Don't stop."

His words made me fuck a little harder and his eyes rolled back in his head, his chest and neck and cheeks flushed red. And the noises he made... sweet mother of God, he moaned with every thrust. I filled his arse and pumped his cock over and over and he raked his hands over his chest, tweaked his own nipple, and his body went rigid. Like a cresting wave, starting in his feet, his second orgasm rolled through him. He arched his back, impaling himself on my cock as he came, almost screaming as he did.

He slumped back on the bed, taking me with him. I was still inside him and I wondered if I should pull out, but he wrapped his long legs around and murmured, "Your turn."

He was so utterly spent and boneless, I sunk deeper inside him. I cradled his head and shoulders. I kissed down his neck and across his jaw until I found his mouth. I rolled my hips thrusting deep inside him and he sucked on my tongue.

And white fire tore painlessly through my body, a pleasure so intense, light danced behind my eyes. The orgasm barrelled me, consumed me, and something changed inside me. My senses returned slowly to the feeling of fingers running through my hair and warm kisses on my neck and shoulder.

"Holy shit."

Griffin croaked out a laugh. "That was incredible for you too, right?"

I pulled back so I could see his face, and it took me a second to focus. "More than that."

The corner of his mouth curled up and he put his hand to my face. "I don't want to ever move."

I took a quick account of my body. "I'm not sure I can."

He chuckled and I slowly pulled out of him, then I wrapped him up in my arms and rolled us onto our sides so I didn't crush him. He ran his hand through my hair and stared into my eyes. Neither of us spoke, just stared, for the longest time. And I'm pretty sure if, years from now, someone were to ask me the moment I knew I was falling in love with Griffin Burke, it was right then.

―――――

I WOKE up to the feel of Griffin peeling himself away from me, then a soft kiss to my temple as he got out of bed, and I smiled as I rolled over. I heard Griffin open the door and let Wicket outside, talking to him as they both went downstairs. I checked my phone; it was seven forty. As much as I hated waking up, I had to admit, waking up with him was pretty damn cool.

I smiled at the ceiling for a few minutes, then rolled out of bed to make us some coffee. By the time they came back inside, I handed him a cup.

"Morning," he said. "Wasn't expecting you to be up yet."

"Someone woke me," I replied with a smile.

He nodded toward Wicket. "Someone needed to pee."

I went to the living room and sat on the sofa with my coffee. Wicket followed, and I got happy kisses from him until Griffin sat beside me, then Wicket thanked him for taking him outside.

"Did you have anything you wanted to do this morning?" he asked.

"Breakfast."

He grinned at me. "You struggle in the mornings, don't you?"

I made a pouty face. "I'm up and made you coffee."

He sipped it. "And it's good coffee, too."

"I just usually take a little while to come to grips with the world." I sipped my coffee. "What about a walk to the park or something?"

"Sounds great." Wicket plonked himself down next to me, put his head on my thigh, and closed his eyes. Griffin gave him a gentle pat and rested his head on the back of the sofa and smiled at me. "But this is kinda great too."

Eventually we did take that walk, just a slow stroll to the park where we sat on a bench seat and watched Wicket explore while we chatted and enjoyed the sunshine. Griffin wore shorts and a singlet top with thongs and sunnies, and he looked so relaxed and handsome, I had trouble looking away. He caught me staring and gave me a shy smile. "See something you like?" he asked.

I didn't look away. "Yep."

He just grinned, took my hand, and looked out over the park. "I have to say, moving here was one of the best decisions I've ever made."

"I'm glad you did."

He squeezed my hand. "So, what have you got planned for this afternoon?"

"Laundry, which is very exciting. And possibly a nap on the couch."

"Sounds good."

"What about you?"

"Much of the same. And groceries, if I plan to eat this week."

"Oh, yeah, I need to do that too." I sighed. "We're such party animals."

He chuckled. "Laundry, groceries, and a nap. I'm pretty sure Bernice and K have a better social life than us. She mentioned a music festival that's on at Kings Beach in a few weeks. I can just picture them sitting on a picnic blanket, beers and hash brownies in hand."

That made me laugh. "We could go too, if you want? That's in Caloundra. We could stay at my parents' place." Then I realised that I just mentioned meeting the parents... "If you want to, that is. Or we could stay somewhere else. It's no big deal."

He squeezed my hand, then threaded our fingers properly. He seemed to think about his next words and I almost apologised before he said, "I'm down with meeting your folks. And I love music festivals."

Relief poured over me like a bucket of water and I barked out a laugh. "Jesus, I didn't really think about how that sounded," I said, letting out a deep breath. "And I know this is all moving really fast, but I'm completely okay with that."

He leaned in and kissed me softly. "I'm completely okay with that too."

My heart knocked against my ribs, and I smiled like an idiot as Griffin got up to chase after Wicket with his leash. "Oh, no you don't. You're not running away again." He caught him easily and they both came back smiling. "Ready to go back?"

I really wasn't ready at all. I wanted this moment to last forever. "If I have to."

We walked back to his place, and after some more making out, on the couch this time—so Wicket got used to us lying together, Griffin had said—I couldn't put off reality any longer and eventually had to go home.

I had Wicket and my overnight bag and stood at his door, trying to find the will to leave. "When will I see you next?" Griffin asked with his big puppy-dog eyes.

"Well, we're both busy with work all week, and Thursday the store is open later, so maybe Friday night?"

Griffin sighed. "That's so far away."

I pulled his chin down so I could kiss him. "It'll go fast."

He didn't look convinced. "I could drive down on Friday after work, and we could get takeout? Or you could cook for me," he suggested with a smile.

"Mmm, I don't know," I pretended to have to think about it. "Will you be staying the night?"

He cradled my face in his hand and slowly covered my mouth with his, tilting his head and kissing me so slow and thoroughly, I dropped my bag and melted into him. My God, he could kiss... When he pulled away, it took me a second to focus. I was breathless, my head was swimming, and my dick certainly liked where that kiss was leading.

"I think that's a yes," he whispered. "Now you better go, or we'll end up back in bed and no one'll be doing laundry."

I think I groaned. Fuck. I gave my dick a squeeze. "Yeah, Friday's a great idea."

He picked up my bag and handed it to me, then scooped up Wicket and carried him down the stairs. He kissed me at my car again and smiled as he felt my hard-on against his hip. "Save that for Friday," he murmured.

"God, you're gonna kill me."

His grin was victorious as he walked away, and I drove home, willing my erection away, while grinning like an idiot.

———

LATER THAT NIGHT, he texted me. *Get everything done?*

Yeah. You?

Yep. What are you doing right now?

Watching TV. Julia Roberts is just about to do the 'I'm just a girl' speech to Hugh Grant.

Oh, I love that movie. Which channel?

Ten.

Love the next part in the press conference. Totally cheesy and awesome.

It is

Didn't know you loved rom-coms...

Don't tell anyone but I love them.

We can watch one on Friday night.

I'd prefer to do something else ;) but if you insist on watching television...

I'm so up for that.

What do you want me to cook for dinner on Friday? I do a mean grilled chicken salad.

Sounds great.

Wicket says thanks for the great weekend.

Just him?

Me too.

Can't wait for Friday. And this weekend you can show me around Maroochydore.

Deal.

Goodnight, Dane.

Night.

I wanted to hug my phone but didn't. Instead I smiled at the TV until the credits for *Notting Hill* were finished.

———

I HAD every intention of texting Griffin on Wednesday after work, but I had to walk Wicket, so I called him instead. "Hey, you."

"Hey, you too."

God, his voice sent a thrill through me. "How was your day?"

"Pretty good. How was yours?"

"Yeah, okay. I'm just out taking his royal highness for a walk."

He snorted. "I won't tell him you called him that."

"I'm pretty sure he'd approve."

"Does he expect people to stand on the side of the road and wave?"

"I'm sure if you suggested it..."

"Oh my God, at work today we had this couple who expected the royal treatment..." He proceeded to tell me about his day and I told him about mine.

"Li, wanted to know if my good mood had anything to do with the tall, handsome guy who came into the store on Friday to give me his address."

He laughed. "What did you tell her?"

"I said it sure did. I refused to give her details though."

"Probably a good idea not to," he said happily.

On Thursday night, he called me. "Hey," he greeted me warmly. Then, "Oh, where are you?"

"At the supermarket. Just grabbing some fresh chicken and stuff for a salad for tomorrow night."

"Ah. Do I need to bring anything? Drinks? Condoms? Lube?"

I laughed so hard in line at the deli that people turned to stare. "No, I'll grab some while I'm here."

He chuckled, warm and throaty in my ear. Then he said, "Just so you know, I prefer silicone based lubes, glycerine-free."

"Duly noted."

I could tell he was smiling by the tone in his voice. "What's the matter? Sound a little flustered."

"Um, I'm in the line at the deli."

He laughed. "Then I better let you go. Just remember, silicone, extra slippery. You can pick your favourite brand of condoms. It'll feel good for me whichever brand you choose."

I made a high-pitched whine just as it was my turn to be served. "Yes, can I please have two full chicken breasts, thank you."

Griffin laughed in my ear. "Boy, I bet that was awkward."

"I'm going now," I mumbled, and he was still laughing when I ended the call.

I took my chicken, grabbed all the salad stuff, picked two bottles of lube—silicone, glycerine-free, thank you, Griffin—and two twelve-packs of condoms, and went home. I was definitely going to have to jerk off before tomorrow night or I'd come as soon as he kissed me.

———

FRIDAY DRAGGED. Like, really dragged. I think everyone in Maroochydore chose that as their "I'm going into the Telstra store to make someone's life miserable" day. By the time I had the shop shut down, I was dying to leave, and I was also late.

Griffin was leaning against his car outside the front of my house, and when I pulled into my driveway, he walked over to meet me. He was still wearing his work uniform, looking sharp as hell with his suit and perfectly up-styled hair. "Thought I had the wrong house."

"Sorry. Shit day. Thought it would never end."

He frowned and leaned in close. "Then we better get inside so I can make it better for you."

My dick started to harden. Oh yeah. If I hadn't jerked off last night, I wouldn't have even made it inside without embarrassing myself.

I fumbled with the key to get in and was met by a tail-wagging Wicket doing his whole body-wiggle, twice over when he saw Griffin follow me in.

Griffin put an overnight bag on the dining table and a grocery bag on the kitchen bench. "Nice place."

"Oh, thanks." I ignored the stifling sexual tension and showed him my house. It wasn't huge, with just one open-plan living area, combined kitchen and dining, and two bedrooms. But it was neat and tidy. Although just a rental, it was, for all intents and purposes, home. "My room, spare room. Bathroom's in here." I took him back to the kitchen. "And there's an outside undercover area."

Griffin looked at my face, then at the bulge in my pants. He met my eyes again and smirked, then went to the grocery bag. "I bought a few things for breakfast. Figured if you were doing dinner, it was the least I could do. And I bought this." He pulled out a chew stick for Wicket. "Thought it might keep him busy for a while."

He unwrapped it, not taking his eyes off me, and held it down for Wicket to take. "Be a good boy and run along. Daddy needs some personal time."

Wicket took it and ran out through his doggy door, and Griffin led me to the couch. He pushed me so I sat down, then he knelt between my legs. "If you're going to make me come twice tonight, and I'm pretty sure you will...," he purred. He unzipped my fly, left my button done up, but pulled out my cock through the opening. "Then it's only fair if you do too."

I pushed my arse forward a little and widened my knees, and he fisted my shaft and slipped his lips over the head. "Oh God, Griffin." Then he proceeded to suck me into oblivion, pumping and licking and swallowing around me, until I came down his throat.

We did manage to cook and eat dinner, give Wicket a short walk around the block, then we cozied up on the sofa for a bit until Griffin decided it was his turn. Then he led me to my room and stripped off his clothes like he was putting on a show. He was so sexual and so damn cheeky. I loved it.

He positioned himself in the middle of my bed and began to stroke himself. He smirked at me. "Remember, before and during."

"How could I forget," I murmured, following him onto the bed.

He was right about that, though. If I was going to come twice that night, then it was only fair he did too.

And he did. I wrung that second orgasm out of him until he was shaking and moaning, writhing and begging, until we both collapsed in each other's arms and didn't move until morning.

———

GRIFFIN MADE ME BREAKFAST, and with a promise to see me on Sunday night and a kiss goodbye, we left for work. I was on cloud nine all damn day, not even the shittiest of customers could deflate my mood. I still wouldn't give Li any more details, much to her annoyance, but then my mum called when I was driving home.

"How've you been? Haven't heard from you in a few days."

"Sorry, been busy."

"Well, your father's knee's much better. He's allowed to drive again this week."

"That's good," I said. I knew how much it'd been driving him insane. "You know he'll want to do everything now and overdo it."

"Oh yes. I've told him that."

"Mum, can I ask you something?"

"Yes, of course, love."

"How did you know?"

"How did I know what?"

"When you met Dad. How did you know he was the one you were going to marry?"

Silence for a beat. "Oh my... Who is he, and when do we get to meet him?"

CHAPTER THIRTEEN

GRIFFIN

I ARRIVED at Dane's place on Sunday night a little after six. The roller door was up so I could see his car in the garage. I'd been looking forward to seeing him since I left his place yesterday morning. I couldn't get enough of him, in and out of the bedroom.

He told me he recognised we were moving pretty fast but he liked it, and I told him I agreed. Wholeheartedly. Literally.

As in, with my whole heart. Sure, I'd had infatuations before and relationships my young heart had thought were love. That was love, to me, at the time.

But this was different. This was butterfly-inducing, blood-warming, heart-skipping. This was the beginning of something very special.

Was it love? Was I ready to call it that? Was I ready to hand over my heart to a guy I'd only known for a few weeks?

Or maybe the better question was, did I even have a choice?

I wasn't going to question it, though, that was for sure. I

was going to enjoy every second, and from the way Dane looked at me, the way he held me, the way he made love to me, told me he felt the same.

He wanted me to meet his parents, for fuck's sake. Well, he kind of said it all wrong, but he didn't retract it when he had the chance. And I didn't lie when I said I was happy to meet his folks.

I mean, if we were really moving fast—dating, boyfriends—then why not? Wasn't that what boyfriends did? And anyway, the music festival was a few weeks away yet, so there was plenty of time to get used to the idea.

I knocked on the front door, expecting a gorgeous Dane and a warm hug and a deep kiss, but was met with... a man who *had* to be Dane's father.

Holy shit. So much for a few weeks. "Um, hi," I said, aiming for happy, hoping like hell he didn't think the overnight bag meant... well, what an overnight bag meant. "Is Dane in?"

"Yes, yes," he said, opening the door. "Come on in." He opened the door, and it was then I realised he had a walking stick and a long purple scar down his knee. "He's out the back. You must be Griffin."

So, Dane had told them about me...

I put my bag down near the door. "Yes, Griffin Burke," I said, shaking his hand.

"Terry Hughes," he said. Then he nodded toward the backyard. "Just so you know, Dane told his mum all about you, and well, she had to meet you. I'm pretty sure he's horrified, but she wouldn't be swayed."

I laughed at that. "If my parents lived closer, I'm sure my mum would've done the same." Which would be true, if I'd told them about him. Which I hadn't. Not in great detail, and I couldn't help but wonder why. I'd told Mum I'd met someone but didn't want to jinx anything by spilling details, but I hadn't mentioned him since.

Then the back sliding door opened and Wicket came bouncing in, straight over to me. "Hey, little man," I said, picking him up. And then a woman came in, petite with pretty red hair, and Dane followed behind her giving me an I'm-so-sorry look all over his face. I smiled at him, then turned to his mum. "Hello. I'm Griffin."

She put her hands to her face. "Aww, look at you. I can see why Dane is so smitten."

Dane closed his eyes slowly and his shoulders sagged in a horrified kind of way, and Terry groaned behind me. "For God's sake, Marie. Don't embarrass the boy."

I was wearing my work uniform, still with my waistcoat on, and my hair done the way Dane liked it. I couldn't help but chuckle. "I um, I don't always look like this. This is me at work. I'm really more of a shorts and T-shirt kind of guy."

Dane finally came over to me and leaned in, kissing my cheek. "Hi," he said, but there was "Oh my God, I'm so sorry" in his eyes.

I really liked the way he kissed me hello in front of his family. "Hey," I replied, with "It's fine" in my smile.

"Did you want to change?" he asked. "Mum and Dad were just leaving."

"Oh, you're not staying for dinner?" I asked his Mum.

Dane stared at the side of my head and I fought a smile. Dane's voice bordered on pleading. "No, Dad's just been allowed to drive again after his knee surgery, he probably shouldn't—"

His mum spoke as though Dane wasn't speaking. "Oh, we really shouldn't," she said, in a way that totally meant they were now staying for dinner.

Dane sagged again and Terry laughed. I took my bag

and left to get changed out of my uniform, and I heard Terry say, "Well Marie, he's got you figured out already."

Then I heard Marie say, "Oh, Dane. He's gorgeous."

Dane's reply was strained and somewhat muted. "Please don't embarrass me."

"It's all right son," Terry said. "I won't let her stay long."

I laughed quietly as I undid my waistcoat. This was unexpected, and my plans of spending the evening naked with Dane had been thwarted, but for some strange reason, I didn't mind. I didn't mind at all.

―――――

WE SPENT the evening sitting at the patio table eating Marie's roast chicken pieces and mashed potatoes. "It's nothing fancy," she said modestly.

"Having a mum-cooked meal is always a good thing," I said, and I think I'd won her over with that. I didn't say it to be cheesy, though. I meant it.

"Where's your Mum and Dad?" she asked gently.

I think she thought they were dead or had disowned me or something. "Oh, they live in Brisbane," I explained. "But my mum insisted on weekly dinners. Even when my sister and I moved out, she'd expect us home once a week for dinner. I never could say no. Everyone loves their mum's cooking."

And that led to conversations about families and school and work, and maybe Dane and I learned a bit about each other at the table with his parents that we probably should've already known.

When his parents eventually said goodbye, we waved them off and Dane pulled me against him and kissed my cheek. "Thank you."

"What for?"

"For not bailing. I told Mum about you on the phone yesterday and might have mentioned that you were coming over tonight, and then they just happen to turn up ten minutes before you." He gave me a squeeze. "I'm sorry I sprung it on you like that."

I turned in his arms and kissed him chastely. "It was fine. I didn't mind, and I certainly wouldn't have bailed."

His smile was tender. "I think my mum approves of you. Actually, I think she loves you more than me."

I snorted. "Not likely. But I'm glad I met them. It's done now, and who knows... maybe if we had left it a few weeks, I'd have been too nervous in the build-up. Being blindsided has its perks."

He sighed deeply and pulled me a little bit tighter. I loved the way our bellies pressed together, flat and warm. He nudged his nose along my jaw and I knew where he was heading with that.

"Can we talk?" I blurted out before he could get too far.

He froze and pulled back warily, with a sad frown. "Oh."

I rolled my eyes. "Not that kind of talk, jeez. I just met your parents!" I took his hand and pulled him over to the couch, and together we sat, holding hands. He felt rigid, so I leaned in and kissed his lips. "Not that kind of talk, I promise."

He let out a breath. "Okay."

"Seriously though, I want to talk. Falling into bed with you is so easy, and—" I let out a low whistle. "—really good. Actually, it's better than really good." I felt the need to fan my face but resisted. "But I don't want it to be just physical. And talking with your parents tonight made me realise there's probably a bunch of stuff about each other, important stuff, that we don't know."

He relaxed then, and a smile tugged at his lips. "You kinda scared me."

"I'm sorry. I didn't mean to blurt it out like that, but with you kissing my jaw... If I'd waited till you got to my ear, we'd be in bed right now."

He chuckled, but then sobered a little. "But we should talk, you're right. If this is going to last, we need to talk." Then, palming his dick, he readjusted himself. "My body just seems to have this ever-present problem when I'm with you."

"Well," I allowed with a smirk, "there are no rules to say we can't talk with you between my legs."

He laughed but, in no time, had me on my back on the couch, my head on the cushion, and he was planted between my thighs. He settled his weight on me and smiled. "So, what did you want to know about me?"

I resisted the urge to moan and roll my hips. "First kiss."

"Penny Ying. Year four."

"A girl?"

"She lost a bet with Toby Shelton and so she had to kiss me." He smiled. "It wasn't terrible but kinda reaffirming for me because I wished like hell Toby had lost. Who was your first kiss?"

I chuckled. "Patrick Dobrev. Year eight, after soccer practice."

"You played soccer?"

"For a few years, during school. Never took it too seriously though. What about you? Play any sport?"

"Rugby league in high school. Surfing."

"We still have to have those surfing lessons."

He kissed me. "We do."

"Next Monday, maybe?"

He nodded just as Wicket came over to inspect what we were doing. "I think he's getting used to us touching," he mused. "But we should probably keep up the desensitising."

"We totally should." I shifted my hips a little to get more comfortable, and Dane reacted in kind by arching into me and shuddering.

"Sorry," he whispered. "I'm trying to behave myself here."

I chuckled. "You're being a very good boy."

He pretended to growl at me but kissed me. "Have you travelled much?"

Oh, right. Question time. "In Australia, I've been to Melbourne, Sydney, and Adelaide. Overseas, I've been to New Zealand for two weeks with the fam, and we went to Bali for schoolies. What about you?" I leaned up and pecked his lips with mine.

"Not much. The Whitsundays, we did an Outback tour with high school and went to Uluru and to Sydney. Overseas, I've been to Fiji. That's it."

"If you could pick any country to go to, where would you choose?" I ran my hand down over his arse.

I saw his restraint flicker in his eyes. "Are you changing the rules of the game?"

I lifted one knee a little higher. "No, just enhancing it. I seem to have the same problem around you."

He ground against my hard-on. "I can tell."

I bit back a groan and pulled his lips to mine before pulling him back. "Dream holiday destination?"

"Inside you," he murmured and crushed his lips to mine. He kissed me deeply, tangling our tongues and rubbing his erection against mine. I couldn't help it, but I cried out, groaning at the contact, and Wicket let out a sharp bark right next to us.

Startled, we broke apart and looked down at the little dog who was watching us, confused. "It's okay, I'm not hurting him," Dane said breathily. He was leaning up on his hands now, our hips still pressed together, and I felt him twitch against me.

"Not yet," I said with a pained laugh. I reached over and ruffled the fur on Wicket's forehead. "But I think your daddy should take me into his bedroom where he can make me scream without scaring you."

Dane was up and off me in a flash, pulling me to my feet. "Bedtime, Wicket," he said, flipping the lights off as he led me to his room. He closed the door behind us and turned to me. His eyes were dark and predatory. "I won't ever hurt you," he whispered, pulling my shirt off. "But you might very well scream."

I grinned and he pounced on me, kissing my mouth, my jaw, my ear. He hoisted me up easily and I wrapped my legs around him and he lowered me to the bed. "Lights on or off?"

"On. I don't want to miss a thing."

His grin was wicked, and he pulled my shorts and briefs off. "Believe me, you won't."

———

WE SPENT the whole of the next day doing sightseeing stuff because Dane wanted to show me around Maroochy-dore, his hometown. We took Wicket with us, of course, going to the beach, the river, and back to Point Cartwright lookout. We ate fresh seafood on the beach, and we laughed at Wicket, who desperately wanted to bring home a piece of driftwood so big it wouldn't fit in the car.

That night, we played more question games on the couch, which ended up with us in bed and naked, sated and sleepy. And on Tuesday, which was our Sunday, the three of us took a drive into the hinterland and found ourselves at the Eumundi markets.

We strolled through the stalls, hand in hand, without a care in the world. We chatted with the stall-owners and Dane found a leather bracelet that matched mine. Simple, thin, plaited black leather with a small metal clasp with rings of pride colours. He put it on his right wrist and something beamed from within him. "Looks perfect," I whispered.

I was pretty sure he wanted to kiss me, right there in front of a hundred other shoppers, but he squeezed my hand instead, and his grin said everything he couldn't.

I found an organic pet treat stall and bought ridiculously priced chew treats for Wicket.

"You don't have to pay for things for him," Dane said.

"These are in my best interest as well," I assured him and showed him the packaging. "It says right here it'll keep him entertained for hours."

Dane laughed and turned to the sales lady. "I'll have two more, please."

We sat in the park and ate frozen yoghurt while Wicket had an organic dog cookie, and reluctantly, we knew we had to go home. "I still have to mow Bernice's lawn," I said. "And do all the boring household things I need to do."

Dane sighed. "Me too. Want me to come over to your place on Friday after work? We can alternate Fridays, like a mid-week thing, and then our weekends, if you want?"

I nodded. "I want."

He smiled, then looked out over the park, at the kids playing and the people enjoying the warm summer day. "You know, since I met you, I've spent more time outdoors than I have in a long time. I mean, I would always walk Wicket, but *actually* getting out and doing stuff."

"Is that a good thing?" I asked. He looked pensive, so I couldn't be sure...

"It's a very good thing." His gaze shot to mine and something settled between us, like doubt had flitted away, leaving only something solid and rare to fill the space that remained.

I couldn't look away, and the *L* word squeezed my heart and tingled on the tip of my tongue, but I stopped it. It was too soon and I didn't want to scare him or risk crushing the hope love had to bloom. If reality was the axe yet to fall, why be the one to hold it? I'd told my mother I didn't want to jinx anything, but was that what I was truly afraid of? Or was it because telling her made it real?

Maybe it was about time I put my heart on the line, for real. For keeps.

I let out a nervous breath. "This is a very good thing."

His blue eyes bore into mine and he nodded. "It really is."

A squealing kid running past startled us both and the moment was broken. *Jesus.* But we walked to his car, and on the drive back to Dane's place, I made a call I knew I had to make.

"Hey, Mum, it's me," I said into my phone.

Dane squeezed my free hand and kept it on his thigh.

"Oh, hi, love. How's things?"

"Yeah, things are great." I swallowed hard. "Um, remember how I told you I met someone?" I looked at Dane and rolled my eyes, trying not to let my nerves get the best of me.

"Yes," she said slowly, cautiously.

"I didn't want to tell you anything about him in case it jinxed everything, but I think we're past that. His name is Dane Hughes, and I don't want you to overreact because I've never introduced you to anyone I've dated, well apart from Nick, but you already knew him, but Mum, I think you should meet Dane." There was a moment of utter silence. Dane frowned and my nerves were making me nauseous. "Mum?"

Then she sobbed into the phone, and I grinned with relief. I put the phone to my chest and looked at Dane. "She's crying."

"Good tears?"

"Are they good tears, Mum?"

More sobbing and a sniffly, "Oh honey, of course."

I nodded to Dane. "Good tears."

He sighed and squeezed my hand. "Oh, thank God."

———

WHEN I FINISHED MOWING Bernice's lawn, it was steaming hot and muggy as hell, so I took my shirt off and wiped down my face with it. She came out with a tall drink of mineral water, so I sat at her table with her. "Here you go. It's too hot to be doing it in the afternoons," she said, scolding me gently.

"I was busy yesterday morning, sorry."

"Oh, yes. All loved up with Mr Wonderful."

I grinned as I sipped my drink. "Something like that."

She smiled but then pointed to my chest. "Well, don't be going around without a shirt and sunscreen, you hear? I know young people think they're invincible. I was the bloody same and look at where it got me." She pointed to the scars that ran from her neck down her arm. "Too many years in the sun and it almost killed me. Melanoma don't give one shit how old you are, boy."

Okay, wow. I'd wondered what the scars were from but had never been game to ask. "Melanoma?"

She nodded. "Doctors took it out, so I guess I count myself as lucky. But the cancer took much more than that. My arm, my career."

God, I didn't know what to say. "I'm sorry to hear that. But I'm glad you're still here to lecture me about it." I gave her a smile, aiming for funny.

"Yeah, well, someone has to," she said bluntly. "Now put your bloody shirt back on."

I snorted but did what I was told. I was out of the sun, technically, but I guessed Bernice didn't exactly care for technicalities.

"That's better," she said, nodding to herself. "Now, when are you seeing this fella of yours again? Just so I know when I need to crank up the tunes again."

I laughed, not even embarrassed this time. "Uh, Friday. And again next Monday and probably Tuesday."

"Oh, so I better get my playlists ready early, huh?"

I grinned. "Probably. We were gonna try and get in that surfing lesson on Monday if you're still interested…"

"Said I would. I'll check what K's doing. He'll probably want to come along, teach you young'ns how it's done. He can still ride a longboard like it's 1973."

"A longboard? Really?"

"Hell, yes. Best there ever was." She got some distant look in her eyes like her memories were playing behind them, and she smiled.

"Can I ask you something?"

Her smile became a little guarded, but she replied, "I dunno. Can you?"

I ignored her gibe at my grammar. "You and K... are you *together* together?"

She sighed. "As much as we'll ever be, I suppose."

"Do you want to be?"

"He does. But I'm happy here on my own." Her words said one thing, but the sadness in her eyes said something else. Before I could say anything, a beeping sound came from her kitchen. "Shit, my brownies," she said, getting up and rushing inside. "Nearly burnt m' brownies."

I followed her inside and watched as she took a tray of brownies out of the oven. "Oh boy, you'd have been in trouble if I'd wasted a whole batch of hash because we were out there yammering."

I smiled at her. "They look okay."

She patted the middle of the brownies, then looked up at me and smiled. "Wanna try one?"

"No thanks," I said with a laugh. "But I tell you what, how about I bring down a barbeque chook and salad for dinner? I have to go to the supermarket so I can pick it up fresh."

She stood up straight. "Will there be any more personal questions about K and me?"

I laughed. "Nope."

"Then sure, why the hell not?"

CHAPTER FOURTEEN

DANE

"HOW WAS DINNER WITH BERNICE?" I asked. I'd just got home from work and was taking Wicket for a walk when my phone rang. Griffin's name on the screen had me smiling even before I'd heard him speak.

His laughter down the phone made me grin. "Oh my God. She's so funny. She thinks she overdid the hash butter or K gave her some extra strong shit because one brownie and she was smashed."

I snorted. "It cracks me up that she's a pothead."

"She says it's for medicinal purposes," he explained. "But I reckon she's been self-medicating since the seventies, at least."

That made me laugh. "She's a riot, that's for sure."

"She said she's good for our surfing lesson this Monday too, if you're still up for it. She was going to ask K and let me know. Apparently K's really good at surfing, and she said with her arm not being much good, we'd be better learning from him."

"Sounds good. Though, you know, I can actually surf..."

"Yeah, I know, but she offered and I think it makes her feel useful or something. I don't know."

"Yeah, I'm not complaining. If not a great lesson in surfing, it'll be funny."

He chuckled. "Yeah. I asked about her and K. She was weird about it, though. Said it was her that put up the boundaries, and when I asked why, she kind of shut the whole subject down. It was weird. I don't know why, I just assumed he was happy living the forever-bachelor life and called around when it suited him. But apparently it's the other way around."

"Maybe she likes her freedom."

"Yeah, maybe. There was something off about it though. Like she wanted it but didn't want to admit she wanted it."

"Oh, look out. Griffin the matchmaker is on the job," I joked.

"Ha! You've met her, right. If Bernice doesn't want to budge, then I don't think even an earthquake could make her move."

"True." I chuckled. "How was work today?"

"Really good. I'm loving it so far. The staff are great, the bosses are good. They like me, so that helps."

I snorted. "Of course they do."

"Yeah, well, I'm a bit of a stickler for professionalism. It either pisses people off or they love it."

"It'd only piss off the people who tend to slack off, wouldn't it?" I asked. "I know in the shop, if I've gotta remind people of rules and procedures, it's because they've gotten complacent."

"Exactly! There's one guy, Brian. I thought he was going to be a problem, but since we cleared the air in the beginning, he's actually turned into one of the guys I can rely on."

"Mmm, is this Brian someone I should be worried about?"

He laughed at that. "Only if I had a thing for over-fifty, silver daddies, whose idea of a fun weekend is knitting and jigsaw puzzles."

I smiled. "Not your thing?"

"No, I prefer my men to take me on surfing lessons and hikes with their cute pup."

My grin was back. "Just as well I know someone like that."

He snorted. "Oh, who knows? Maybe Brian is the kinkiest one at the Sunshine Coast BDSM club. I really have no idea, and I have nothing against knitting and jigsaw puzzles. Actually, I don't mind doing jigsaw puzzles. My nan always has one half-done on her dining table and I'd help her every time we called in. But I do like being... more active."

His tone didn't go unnoticed. The innuendo didn't either. "I know you do. You like it more active several times a night." Mental images of him impaled on my dick, writhing and coming, and that sexy moan of his flashed through my mind.

He laughed warmly. "That I do. Just as well I know someone who can keep up with that."

"God, I shouldn't be thinking about that... Do you know how hard it is to walk with a hard-on?"

His laugh sounded a little strained. "At least I'm on my couch and can take care of mine."

Then I heard a familiar slicked friction sound. "Oh fuck," I whispered. "Are you...?"

"You started it," he said, his voice gravelly.

"I'm walking in a public park," I hissed, willing my dick

not to listen. "Do you want me to get arrested for lewd behaviour?"

He moaned through a laugh. "No, I want you to go home so you can talk me through this orgasm."

I turned on my heel, pulling Wicket back the way we'd come. "I can be home in five minutes."

The slicked friction noise sounded more frantic. So did his voice. "Make it three."

"I'll call you back," I said and ended the call. "Come on, Wicket. Let's run."

Two minutes and forty-three seconds later, I called him back. He answered with, "Oh, thank God. I'm close."

Oh fuck. He was insatiable.

I unclipped Wicket's leash and locked myself in the bathroom. I considered putting the phone on speaker, but I wanted the closeness of his voice, his grunts, in my ear. Still fully dressed, with my sneakers on and my phone pressed to my ear and leaving the water shut off, I stepped into the shower. With my free hand, I pulled my erection out of my shorts and stroked, desperate for friction.

"Your panting sounds so hot," he murmured.

"You made me run home."

He groaned. "I can't get enough of you. I think about you all day."

"You're killing me," I said, stroking myself harder. Precome slicked the head, and each pass made a wet sucking noise that echoed in the bathroom.

"I can't wait for Friday night." His pitch was higher. He was so close, I could tell. I knew that tone. "For what you'll do to me."

"I'll bury my cock inside you and make you come so hard."

"Oh fuck," he groaned, an almost painful sound.

The sound of him coming hurtled me to the edge. "Oh, Griffin."

"Oh yeah," he rasped. "I can almost feel you in my arse."

And that was all it took. I sprayed the tiles with my release, not even aware of the sounds coming from my throat until the echo boomed in the small room.

"Holy shit, Dane," Griffin whispered.

All I could do was moan and rest my forehead on the tiles.

"Are you okay?" he asked, sounding half-amused, half-concerned.

"I think I died and heaven is a room that looks some-what like my bathroom."

He laughed. "Okay, so that was seriously the hottest thing ever."

"It kinda came from nowhere." At least the room wasn't spinning anymore. I tucked myself back in and winced as my sensitive cock objected to my briefs and shorts. I toed out of my sneakers, suddenly feeling overheated. I put the toilet lid down and sat on it. "God, I need to sit down before I have a shower, or something. I think you broke me."

He chuckled. "I'll fix you right up again on Friday night."

I gave a groany chuckle. "Oh, I'm sure you will."

"I better get cleaned up."

"Me too." *Well, me and the shower.* I pulled off a shoe, making a start on getting undressed. "Oh, and Griffin?"

"Yeah?"

"I think about you all day too."

———

AT WORK ON THURSDAY, Li spent the entire day side-eyeing me. "Something's different with you. I noticed it yesterday, but I think it's worse today," she said.

"Worse?"

She shrugged. "Or better. Depends if you're a people person."

I snorted. Despite how good at her job she was, she was *not* a people person.

"Haircut?"

"No."

"New moisturiser?"

I squinted at her. "Uh, no."

"Don't underestimate the power of a good moisturiser."

"I'll try not to."

"Have you lost weight?"

I blinked. "Do I need to?"

"No, no," she said quickly. "It's just something's different. Did you use a bronzer?"

"Yep. It's called the sun."

"You have a glow." She studied me for a moment longer, head tilted, then she gasped. "Oh my God."

I touched my nose, wondering if I had a booger or something equally as horrifying. "What?"

"You're in love."

"I am not." It was a lie, and I knew it was a lie as soon as I'd said it. I was struck dumb for a moment, then tried to laugh it off. "Don't be silly."

She sidled up to me. "You totally are."

"I'm... I uh, I don't know what I am."

She didn't say anything for a second, but I couldn't bring myself to look at her. "You're happy, that's what you are. And it's about time." Then she waved her hand like a witch at a cauldron would. "If you like that hearts and mushy stuff, that is."

———

LATER THAT NIGHT, before he could call me and make me run home needing to jerk off, I sent Griffin a text. *Li, at work, thinks I'm a total sap. I blame you.*

Why?

Shit. I hadn't thought ahead, clearly. *Reckons I was staring off into space with a smile.*

Stare into space with a smile often?

Clearly not. Not before you anyway. Hence the blaming.

LOL I'll take the blame for that ;)

I smiled as I typed. *Just about to take Wicket for a walk. He's standing at the door looking at me like I'm a bad parent. Can't wait for tomorrow night.*

You're such a bad daddy... Great. Now I'm thinking about you being a real bad daddy...

LOL I'm walking out the door now. No mad dashes home tonight to take matters into my own hands, okay?

Saving it for tomorrow night? ;)

I groaned. *Yes.*

Oh God. Now I'm thinking about how good that's going to be...

No touching yourself. Save it for me.

His response was immediate. *You're killing me.*

Promise me.

Fine. I promise. But you better be here by five thirty or I'll start without you.

God, I was getting hard already. *Be ready.* Then I added, *Now I'm walking funny. Thanks.*

Haha!

I turned my phone off and grumbled all the way to the park.

———

NEEDLESS TO SAY, Friday knock-off time couldn't come around fast enough. I had the shop closed, all sales processed and data sent to Head Office, and was out the door by 5:05. I was at Griffin's place at 5:25.

I was inside him by 5:40.

And again at 8:30.

Being joined with him, being buried inside him, making love to him, felt like heaven. It felt like home. Fury and tranquillity, all at the same time. An all-encompassing, raging storm and a peaceful summer breeze. He was everything.

And when he clung to me and gasped my name as he unravelled beneath me, surrounding me, he was home, and I never wanted to leave.

———

SATURDAY AFTERNOON DRAGGED despite being busy, and despite my good mood. Li kept rolling her eyes at me, but I couldn't bring myself to care. I was happy. So fucking what.

Even though I'd just seen him this morning—our Friday night, mid-week dates were my new favourite thing—I half expected him to text or call me while I was walking Wicket before dinner, but he didn't. So when I got home, I parked my arse on the couch and hit dial.

"Oh, hey," he said with a sigh.

"Everything okay?"

"Someone gave me a good going over last night," he said dreamily.

"Are you sore?"

"No, just tired."

Oh, thank God. "I was worried there for a second."

"You have no reason to worry. You take good care of me." He still sounded a little off. "But speaking of worried..."

I sat forward. "What's up?"

"Bernice was a little weird this afternoon."

"Was she high?"

"I don't think so. She said her blood sugar's been acting up."

"Is it all the brownies she eats?"

"That's what I said. She needs the medicine or whatever, but she says she won't smoke it too often because of the damage it does to her lungs."

"Can she not get legit medication from a doctor?"

"Medicinal marijuana isn't legal here." He sighed. "And she said the legit meds made her feel sick."

"Just keep an eye on her."

"Yeah, I will."

"Have you got K's number?"

"Nope."

"Well, maybe ask for it tomorrow or something."

"Yeah, I will." He sighed again. "Thank you. I feel better for talking about it."

"You're welcome."

On Sunday morning when I got to work, I sent Griffin a quick message. *Did you see Bernice this morning? How was she?*

His reply came through a few hours later, I assumed

when he was on a break. *Yep. She was having her cuppa outside when I was leaving. She said she felt better.*

That's good. See you tonight.

Can't wait. Two whole days…

It was a little later by the time we got the store closed down and I had to go home first to pick up Wicket, so it was almost six when I arrived at Griffin's. I let Wicket through to the yard and he ran off to scout and sniff, and I took the stairs up to Griffin's flat two at a time. I knocked on his door, and when it opened and I was met with his amazing smile, I had a brilliant idea.

He pulled me in for a kiss and I wrapped my arms around him, sighing as our bodies melded. It was so damn easy being with him; everything physical between us was like left- and right-hand coordination. It was effortless. And we could have easily gone to his bedroom or fallen on the couch, but like he said before, we needed to be more. I broke the kiss and hugged him instead. "I thought we could go out for dinner tonight," I suggested.

He pulled back, keeping his hands on my hips. "Really?"

I smiled at the incredulous look on his face. "Yes, really. Like a date."

His whole face lit up now. "That sounds awesome."

"I haven't made reservations anywhere. I figured we could just walk the esplanade and find a little café somewhere with outside seating so we can take Wicket."

He drew his bottom lip in between his teeth and fought a smile. "If you're trying to be romantic to bed me, mister, you know you don't have to."

I laughed. "I know I don't have to. I just thought it'd be nice. We can actually have a conversation instead of spending the entire time in bed."

He went to the kitchen counter and collected his wallet and keys but then stopped. "But we will be spending the rest of the night in bed, yes?"

I snorted at him. "Ah, yes."

"Good," he said brightly. He pocketed his wallet and phone and jiggled the keys in his hands. "I'm ready to go."

We found a park on David Low Way and walked hand in hand up the beach so Wicket could run himself ragged and then came back down the street that faced the beach. People walked past us, around us when we stopped to look in a store window, and we found a quiet little café across from the surf club. We sat at a table out of the way on the footpath and discussed the menu for a bit. When the waitress came over, he asked for the Mediterranean chicken salad, and I opted for the Thai beef, and two light beers.

There weren't any awkward silences. Griffin launched into a recount of how his day went and I told him about mine. We played the twenty-question game again, this time centred around food, as we waited for our meals to arrive. I learned he hated mangoes and roast pork but loved bacon and ham. He wasn't exactly allergic to mushrooms but would rather die before he ate them, and speaking of death, he could kill for authentic Italian cannoli.

"I'll keep that in mind," I said. "If I need to get in your good books, I'll know what to get you."

"I would love you forever if you did." Then he seemed to realise what he'd just said.

That he'd love me forever.

He balked and blushed, then sipped his drink, but I couldn't let the opportunity pass. I had to say something...

"Is that all it would take?" I whispered.

Before he could reply, with the world's worst timing, the waitress brought our meals to the table. The setting sun had cast a low orange light over us and it made everything look kind of surreal. It sure felt it.

The *L* word had been said, not directly, but now it hung in the air between us like motes on the sunlight, a random trajectory, too afraid to land.

Griffin's eyes met mine and his smile turned shy, and I knew—I just knew—he felt the same. He was in this as much as I was. This incredible, ridiculous thing that we'd found ourselves in. The beginning of something wonderful, of something perfect. Of something permanent.

I was in it, all right. In over my head.

I don't remember actually tasting my dinner. I just kept shoving food in my mouth to stop myself from blurting out nonsensical things that maybe he wasn't ready to hear. Maybe he felt the same, because we ate our meals without speaking. Not an uncomfortable silence, but now it felt like there were unsaid things sitting at the table with us.

When Griffin patted his belly and said he was done, we paid and started the slow walk back to the car. He slipped his hand in mine and sighed. "There's something beautiful about the sound of crashing waves at night time. It's soothing."

I squeezed his hand. "There is."

"Someone at work today asked me what my plans were for my days off," he said. "I told them I was just hanging out with my boyfriend. It was weird to say it out loud for the first time. I'm sure I grinned like an idiot. She probably wondered what was wrong with me."

And there it was. A small validation. A subtle verbalisation of what we'd struggled to say earlier. We wanted to claim this relationship, to tell the world we belonged with each other.

I pulled him close and put my arm around his shoulder

instead. It made my heart soar to hear him call me that. "I sure do like the sound of that."

He slipped his arm around my waist. "Boyfriend?"

"Yep."

"It does sound nice."

We got to the car and I gave him a squeeze before I let go of him. "What does my boyfriend want to do now?" I asked, getting a rush from saying it too.

He pushed me up against the car door. His voice was sexy and his dick pressed against my hip. "I'll give you one guess and one guess only."

I knew damn well what he wanted, but I had to play along. "Can you give me a clue?"

"It involves me being face down on the bed and you trying to fuck me into it."

I swallowed hard. "That's some clue."

He stepped back, opened the passenger door, stopped, and smirked at me. "What are you waiting for?"

I buckled Wicket into his car harness and finally slid into my seat, carefully adjusting myself. Griffin looked at the bulge at my crotch, then to my eyes, and grinned.

"You're sadistic," I said with a smile.

"You can teach me a lesson when you're pummelling me into the mattress."

"And bossy."

"Yes, well," he said, running his hand through his hair. "I told you that. You'll probably get sick of me barking orders at you sooner or later."

I pulled the car out onto the street and took his hand. "I highly doubt that." Then for good measure, I added, "Boyfriend."

He lifted our joined hands to his lips and kissed my knuckles. "Boyfriend."

We got back to his place and went through the side gate like two giggling, and very handsy, schoolboys. Wicket ran off, we realised a little belatedly, to greet Bernice.

"Gee, don't let the audience stop you."

Griffin and I broke apart. He tried to fix his hair and catch his breath. "Oh, hi," he managed. "Didn't see you there."

She laughed. "Clearly not."

"We, uh, we were just heading upstairs," I said, embarrassed. "We've been out for dinner."

"How are you feeling?" Griffin asked.

"Yeah, I'm fine." She waved him off. "Go on up. I'll crank out some tunes so if the neighbours complain, at least it'll be G-rated." She stood up. "Any preferences? I'm in the mood for some Credence. Or what about a seventies remix?"

"Ah, sure. Credence sounds good," Griffin said, fighting a smile. "Um, we still good for that surfing lesson tomorrow? If you want to make it another day or next week, just let me know."

She stopped at her door. "Well, I'll be fine. Whether you'll be able to walk tomorrow is a different story," she said to Griffin. Then she looked at me. "After Friday night, I'm surprised the boy can move. I would ask what the hell it is you do to him, but I really don't think I want to know."

I barked out a laugh, and Griffin covered his eyes with his hand. "Oh God."

I stammered, "I don't... it's not like... he's just vocal." Griffin cringed into my side. For someone taller than me, he could fold himself down to tuck his face into my neck with ease.

Bernice laughed. "So you don't need mood music. You need something with bass. Credence it is then." She put one foot inside, then stopped and looked back at us. "See you both in the morning. What time should I tell K?"

Griffin poked his head around so he could see her. "I'll mow the lawns after breakfast, then we can head down. Then we'll be done in time to buy you both lunch."

"Deal," she said, disappearing inside.

By the time we got upstairs, "Lookin' Out My Back Door" began to play, and we both laughed. Bernice sure had a sense of humour. We didn't get much further than closing the door before we were deep-kissing and hand-roaming. The chemistry between Griffin and me had reduced from sizzling to slow burn, and by the time we were on his bed, "I Put a Spell On You" was playing.

Yeah, Credence Clearwater Revival was a great choice indeed.

———

I SAT with Bernice while Griffin mowed her lawn after breakfast. She was a little quiet but nothing I couldn't put down to a mood and not a health concern. And I hadn't given much thought about where it was I knew her from. She was just Bernice to me now, Griffin's somewhat eccentric, stoner landlady.

Later, we were walking onto the beach. Griffin, K, and I carried boards which K had kindly loaned us for the day. Bernice carried a towel and a tote bag, and Wicket ran ahead down to the water. Then a guy in a wetsuit with a board came out of the ocean and walked past us toward the car park.

He was probably forty, maybe fifty years old. He stopped and stared at Bernice, probably wondering how a small, old woman could wear a huge straw sombrero, and K put his arm around Bernice protectively. She lifted her head high and mumbled something, but they both kept walking.

The surfer guy looked at Griffin and me and grinned. "My God," he said, amazed. "That's Bunny Warren." He shook his head, still smiling and seemingly stuck, like he wasn't sure which way he'd been going.

Griffin frowned and pulled me along, following after Bernice and K. "What the hell was that guy's problem?" Griffin mumbled.

It dawned on me then. "Holy shit. I just realised where I know Bernice from."

CHAPTER FIFTEEN

GRIFFIN

I STOPPED WALKING and stared at Dane. "What?"

"You know before when I said Bernice was familiar but I couldn't place her?"

"Yeah?"

He grinned. "She's Bunny Warren."

"Who?"

"Just the greatest female surfer to ever live."

I blinked. "What?"

"Bunny Warren," he whispered. "I had no idea what her first name was. For all I knew, it could have been Bunny. She's the one who made it on the pro circuit when men told her she couldn't."

It was ringing some distant bell in my memory... "I was never really into surf culture."

"It's a famous story around here. Back in the late seventies, early eighties. She fought for women's surfing, won some title, got some huge sponsorship deal, but disappeared. Never surfed again."

I looked to where Bernice was now straightening a towel out on the sand. She fixed her huge hat to ensure as much of her stayed out of the sun as possible. She was wearing a long-sleeve shirt, which I'd never seen her wear—I'd only ever seen her in singlet style shirts, but she was being very sun-smart today—and her long grey hair was in a single plait down her back.

"The scars down her neck and arm," I said softly. "It was melanoma. She told me. She said the doctors saved her life but took the use of her arm and took her career."

Dane's brow furrowed. "Oh man. That sucks so bad." He looked toward where Bernice and K were.

I put my hand on his arm before he could start walking again. "Don't let on that you know. If she wanted us to know, she'd have told us."

He nodded. "Yeah, of course."

We walked down the hot sand to where they'd set up camp, and Wicket came running over after exploring God knew where. Dane planted his board into the sand, standing it up. "So, how do we start?"

"Lay your boards down," Bernice said. "Griffin needs to learn how to stand before he can surf."

Dane could surf, though it had been years since he'd done it. There had to be a 'like riding a bike' thing for surfing. I mean, surely once you knew how, a muscle memory brought it all back.

But me? I had no clue.

I laid my board down in the sand and gave it a once over, making Bernice snort. "It ain't gonna bite ya."

I cringed. "Just so you know, I have no sense of balance and this might very well be as frustrating for you as humiliating as it is for me."

K looked somewhat pained. "Can you swim?"

"Oh, sure."

His relief was evident. "Okay then. That's a start."

Bernice sat on the towel and gave instructions, while K stood next to me and helped with the logistics of my long limbs. We knelt on the boards, then pretended to be paddling, getting a feel for the side-to-side motion of the board moving under our weight.

Then we had to hold onto the board and jump to our feet. Which sounded easy, and Dane did it easy enough, and K put his board down on the sand next to me to help show me, but for the life of me, I couldn't do it.

After I failed another five times, Bernice stood up, mumbling and cussing at me under her breath. "Get off the board," she said.

I did as I was told and she took my place. She got down on her knees, then using only her right hand, she pushed herself up and got to her feet. "Like that," she said, stepping off the board.

"Oh, okay, because that's not difficult or anything," I said sarcastically.

K grinned at her, a look of wonder on his face. I had the feeling she hadn't stepped onto a board in a long, long time because his expression said as much.

Bernice rolled her eyes and waved him off, sitting back on her towel. "Shut up," she said, fixing her hat.

Still smiling, K showed me again, in slow motion this time, explaining in small steps. "Look around the water. See where the wave's at. Grab the board. Breathe. Hoist up. Feet underneath ya. Don't rush to stand. Get your balance first. Breathe. Stand."

Jesus Christ. K had to be pushing seventy and he was running rings around me. I couldn't give up.

I tried it again and again, and the more tired I got, the harder it became, but after what felt like an eternity, I did it.

I got to my feet and put my hands above my head, like

some kind of victory dance for the lame. "I did it!"

Dane and K laughed, and Bernice rolled her eyes. "Now try doing it in the water."

I looked out to the ocean. "Oh."

K clapped me on the shoulder. "It's not that daunting. Come on. Let's skin this cat."

Skin this cat? "What?"

K laughed. "Sorry. Forgot which generation I'm talking to."

Dane grinned beside me. He looked kinda gorgeous in the bright sunshine with the blue Pacific Ocean rivalling the colour of his eyes. "I have the feeling I'm going to be doing this whether I really want to or not."

"Go on," Bernice said from beneath her huge hat. "What's the worst that could happen? Getting wet?"

"Seeing a shark," I said. "Actually being bitten by a shark." I looked back out to the water. I broke out in a sweat that had nothing to do with the sun. "Jesus. We're not going to see a shark, are we?"

K smiled. "That's the beauty of the Great White. You don't often see them before they get ya."

I took a step back. "Nope."

Dane laughed. "They have nets up. You'll be fine."

K laughed at me. "Honestly, I was just joking. Your biggest worry out there is getting up on your board."

Dane made a face that was half-frowny, half-smiley. "Come on, babe."

"Babe? I'll have you know, babe, if I die a gruesome death from Jaws, I'm gonna be really pissed."

He laughed. "You're cute when you're snippy. So I reckon you'll be hot AF when you're pissed."

K picked up his board, then nodded at ours. "Come on, let's skin this... let's do whatever the kids do these days."

The cool water was a beautiful reprieve from the hot sun and sand, and I managed to carry the board into the water without banging the fins into my shins too much. As soon as it was deep enough, I held the board to my chest and careened onto the surface with more grace than I deserved, and I began to paddle.

Dane, who was paddling on his own board, looked over to me and grinned. The way droplets of water refracted the sunlight off him was glorious and distracting because I watched him nose in under a wave, and before I could think about what he was doing, the same wave dumped me.

I broke the surface, gasping for air and grappling with the board, but managed to haul myself back onto it. Both Dane and K were well ahead of me now, laughing at me.

"Go under the wave," Dane called out.

I shook my hair out. "I would have if you weren't looking so damn hot and distracting me."

Dane laughed and K shook his head, and as soon as we were far enough out, he sat up on his board, feet dangling. He'd taken us to the end of the beach where the beginner surfers could stay out of the way of the better surfers, and the swimmers tended to stay between the flags. Apart from a few other guys, we were completely alone. Thankfully. I didn't fancy failing in front of an audience.

It really was a gorgeous day, though. The sun was beaming, a few white clouds dotted the blue sky, the water was aqua-green and crystal clear.

Then K started counting the waves coming in, telling us to get a feel for the rhythm and explaining which waves were good to surf and which were good to leave alone.

They all looked the same to me.

But then he got up on his knees as a wave rolled in. "Okay, watch this. Start paddling when it's that far away.

Paddle, paddle..." Then he got up to his feet and rode the wave a few metres before careening off the crest, lowered himself back down, and paddled back to us. "Now it's your turn."

Dane went first. He watched, he waited, he counted, then started to paddle like crazy, and got up on his feet. He rode the wave for a good while, making it look easy.

"Yeah!" K said proudly, raising his fist in cheer. Dane paddled back toward us, his face split into a grin.

"Hey, Griffin," K said, snapping his fingers. I went from staring at the sexiness that was Dane and looked at K. "Stop checking out the scenery and watch for your wave."

Oh God, I was actually going to try to surf.

I did as they did. I got up to my knees, I watched, I waited, I started paddling like mad, and the wave took me. I felt the force of the wave lift me, steady the board, and I knew that was the moment I had to get to my feet.

I gripped the board and heaved myself up, bringing my feet in under me. And I stood. Holy shit, I was surfing!

Well, I was surfing for half a second before I lost balance and bit the surface, but for the briefest moment, I was surfing! I broke to the surface and grabbed my board, breathlessly paddling back to Dane and K. I laughed. "Did you see that? I did it!"

"You did good, kid," K said.

Dane was grinning at me, but then he swivelled his head around to look at the shore. "Can you hear that?"

"Hear what?" I asked. I couldn't hear anything, just the sound of my blood pumping in my temples. I shook my head to clear the water from my ears and then a sound carried on the wind.

A dog was barking.

"That's Wicket," Dane said.

K paddled over, studying the shoreline, and the three of us stopped, waited, and listened. It was hard to see because we were quite far out, especially with the rise and fall of the ocean, but on every crest, we could see Wicket facing us, barking.

"That's not his normal bark," Dane said. "Something's wrong."

K sprang into action, belly down, paddling hard, and Dane and I scrambled to follow him. K body-surfed his board into shore, jumped to his feet, and ran through the water up the sand to Bernice.

He was faster than us, but we weren't that far behind him. I could see Bernice was lying back, and she might have looked peaceful, but her leg was bent at an odd angle. Not like she'd lain down, but like she'd fallen back...

"Bernie," K called out. He went to his knees beside her and shook her gently. "Bernie!"

No response.

K shook her a little harder, his voice starting to panic. "Bunny, wake up!"

She stirred but didn't fully come to. K looked up at us. "Call ooo."

But a lifeguard appeared right then and knelt beside her and took immediate action. She had a walkie-talkie and was talking into it, codes or directions for something. "Has she been ill?" the lifeguard asked. "Drinking?"

We all shook our heads. My heart was pounding. The adrenaline and fear made my hands shake. "She's been feeling off for a day or two," I said. "I think the doctor told her she had to watch her diet. Something to do with blood sugar."

K looked up at me, and it was pretty clear this was news to him.

I shrugged at him. "I don't know any more than that. She wouldn't say."

The lifeguard's walkie-talkie crackled to life and I couldn't hear what it said because Bernice mumbled something, and K cradled her head. "You're such a stubborn old fool," he said, so lovingly and painfully, it hurt my heart.

"Ambulance'll be here soon," the lifeguard said. "Let's get her out of the sun."

K picked her up and carried her off toward the shade near the car park, while Dane picked up Wicket and I collected all our belongings. Sirens wailed in the distance, getting louder, coming faster.

The adrenaline waned and left behind an awful, hollow feeling. Frightening. To see Bernice so weak and ill and to just stand there useless, helpless, was such a horrible situation.

But soon the ambulance arrived. Two guys in uniform met us with a gurney, asked us a few questions we couldn't rightly answer, strapped Bernice in, and loaded her into the ambulance.

"I'm going with her," K said. No one dared argue.

"Which hospital are you taking her to?" I remembered to ask.

"Nambour," one paramedic replied.

I gave K a nod. "We'll see you there."

They left, and as soon as they were out of the car park, the sirens started again, this time fading as they got further away.

Dane, who had Wicket now tucked under one arm, patted me with his free hand. "Come on. Grab the boards. Let's go."

Of course. Yes. God, it felt like I was stuck, but his reminder made me move. A small crowd had gathered around, and one guy had kindly brought our boards up. "Thank you," I said to him, grabbing them and loading them into the back.

Dane held onto Wicket and climbed into the passenger seat. "Should we go home first? Drop Wicket and the boards off. They won't let us in to see her straight away," he said calmly, giving my knee a squeeze.

"Yeah, good idea." They certainly wouldn't let us in to see her if we had a dog with us. I gave Wicket a pat. "You knew something was wrong, didn't you, buddy?"

He stood on Dane's leg, his little tongue lolling out of the side of his mouth, looking rather pleased with himself. Dane gave him a hug. "You did good today, hey, little guy."

I drove straight to my place because it was quicker than going down to Dane's. I put the boards in the garage and let Wicket into my place. Dane made sure he had water and gave him one of those organic chews, and with a promise to see him again soon, we left.

I didn't know how to get to Nambour, so Dane drove my car. It wasn't that far, maybe fifteen–twenty minutes, but it felt like ages. I stared out at the scenery, cane fields giving way to houses as we got closer.

"Do you think she'll be okay?" I asked.

Dane took my hand. "I'm sure she will." Whether he believed it or just said it to make me feel better, I wasn't sure.

"Thank God Wicket was there," I mumbled.

Dane smiled and squeezed my hand. "Yeah. He's pretty smart."

"If it weren't for him, I'd hate to think what would have happened to Bernice."

"She'll be okay," he offered, but the truth was, that was something he just couldn't know.

We arrived at the ER and were told she was being seen by the doctors and that we would have to sit and wait. So, we sat and we waited. And if the drive to the hospital took ages, being in that God-awful waiting room felt like an eternity. We sat in the plastic chairs and stared at the scuffed wall opposite us. "Do they make these chairs uncomfortable on purpose?" I griped, shifting in my seat again. It didn't help that we were still wearing our boardies and I had sand in places it didn't strictly belong.

Dane gave me a sympathetic smile. "I think so."

"And why do all hospitals smell like hospital food and disinfectant and vomit?"

I was being testy and he, with the patience of a saint, took my hand. "She'll be okay."

"Can you believe she's some world-famous surfer chick from the seventies?" I asked.

He nodded and smiled. "You know what? I really can."

"I knew she'd lived an interesting life, but I had no idea." I sighed. "I guess when you think you know someone, you really don't."

Dane squeezed my hand and nudged his arm into mine. "Yes, you do. She's probably told you more about the real her than she has anyone else."

I thought about that, closed my eyes and let my head fall back, but I never let go of his hand.

"And I reckon I know you pretty well," he murmured. "Even though we haven't known each other all that long, we know each other, don't we?"

Still leaning against the wall behind me, I turned my head to look at him. "Yeah, I reckon we do."

Then a woman in scrubs came out into the waiting room and everyone paused, waiting... She read the sheet of paper in her hand. "Griffin Burke?"

Dane and I both stood. "That's me," I said.

"You can come through now," she said, leading us through the triage doors. We followed her down a hall of cubicles and she stopped at one near the end and put her hand on the curtain. She gave us a nod and told us in a curt tone, "You've got ten minutes."

Bernice lay in bed, looking different from the Bernice I was used to seeing. She had tubes taped to her hand, monitor pads stuck to her chest, she was pale, and her grey hair lay in waves around her shoulders. She appeared softer somehow. K sat in a chair beside the bed, and the poor guy looked like he'd had ten years taken off him.

"Hey," I said gently. "Up for visitors?"

Bernice smiled. "I told them they best go find you."

"How're you feeling?" I asked.

"Better now," she said, though considering she'd been unconscious before, that was hardly surprising.

"What did the doc say?" I pressed.

"Blood sugar." Bernice rolled her eyes. "I'm fine."

"She's not fine," K said. "She almost died. She'll need daily injections now. If she'd been home alone and no one had found her, she would have died." Then he looked to her. "You were lucky Wicket the dog was keeping an eye on you."

Bernice smiled at us. "Yes, I hear he's our little hero."

"Do you remember anything?" Dane asked.

Bernice shook her head. "I wasn't feeling too great, but you know, we just soldier on."

"You should have said something," K said before I could.

Bernice went to wave her hand, but it was attached to an IV and she stopped, letting her hand fall back to the bed. She sighed loudly instead.

"What're they doing with you?" I asked. "Do you have to stay?"

"Yeah," she grumbled. "Sleepovers just aren't what they used to be."

"Do you need me to grab you anything from home?" I asked. "I can bring it back."

"Oh, that's really sweet of you," she said.

"I can grab it," K said softly. "I'm coming back anyway." Then K looked to us. "If you boys can take me home, then I can come back with a few of her things."

"You don't need to fuss," she said, her brow creasing.

K scowled at her. "You can stop being so stubborn. I'll fuss if I want to bloody fuss."

She tsked and rolled her eyes. "Still the same after all these years."

"And so are you," he bit back at her. "You'd think after fifty-something years, you'd stop being so damn stubborn."

"You'd think after fifty-something years, you'd know when to quit."

K didn't reply to that, and it was pretty obvious to everyone that her words had hurt him. They clearly had so much history, and I wasn't sure what to make of their bickering.

A doctor came in and read a printout from one machine she was hooked up to. "So, I hear a world-famous surfer is in today?" he asked, giving Bernice a smile.

Her eyes darted to mine like it was a secret she didn't want me to hear. "I already know," I said. "Dane told me."

She looked at Dane, then back to me, then to the doctor. "Well, don't go telling anyone," she barked at him. "I don't need no one sniffing around me for a story, especially when I'm in here."

The doctor—or was he a nurse? I wasn't sure—

pretended to lock his lips and throw away a key, then did another pin prick test on her finger. He seemed happy with the results. "Okay, we've got you a room upstairs. We're gonna get you moved soon, okay?"

She grumbled something just as K said, "Well, Doc, she won't listen to me about someone watching over her, so maybe you can talk some sense into her." K stood up and walked out. "I'll wait outside."

Bernice frowned and the doctor gave her a lecture, I assumed not for the first time, about how it was a good idea, just while she got used to the insulin injections, that someone be there to watch over her.

"I don't need no goddamn babysitter," she barked, then she clammed up.

He obviously knew when a battle couldn't be won. He patted her hand. "We'll chat later."

So, yes, she was being stubborn. I felt kind of awkward just standing there, but I had to do something... "K just wants to help," I offered.

"Well, I've managed this long on my own. I can manage another sixty bloody years on my own."

I didn't need to explain the maths. I knew what she meant. "He was worried sick today. He was scared, Bernice." I frowned. "Like really scared."

"He'll get over it," she added defiantly. Then she sniffed. "He wants me to move in with him or him with me. I don't know. I turned him down."

Oh.

"Oh."

Her eyes shot to mine. "What do you mean 'oh'?"

"Well that explains the look on his face."

"What look?"

"The look that he'd just had his heart broken."

She blinked and went to say something but decided against it and pressed her lips into a thin line.

"Now, I don't know him too well, but I'd say there's a good chance he's been in love with you for fifty-something years."

She frowned and looked away, and I had to remember that she was in hospital, rather unwell. "He doesn't need to be spending his life looking after a cripple," she whispered.

"You're hardly a cripple," I replied.

She rolled her slack shoulder and her left arm moved clumsily. "Ain't real friggin' useful, either."

Oh Jesus. "Is that why you keep turning him away? Because you think you're not able-bodied enough?"

"I'm not who I used to be. Haven't been her for a long time."

"Bullshit." Her eyes went wide and I stared right back at her. "You're still you."

"He fell in love with the surfer-girl all those years ago. Not the one-armed girl."

"No," I said softly. "He fell in love with the girl. Do you think he'd have stuck around all these years if he hadn't?"

She frowned, a little teary, and turned her head.

"I'm sorry," I said. "I don't mean to upset you."

She waved me off with her good arm.

I took a deep breath. "Anyway, K's coming back with your stuff. Is there anything I can tell him to grab you?"

She shook her head sadly. "Just a nightgown or something. And a cardigan. The fucking air conditioning in here is frightful. You'd think they're getting me ready for the fridge slab in the morgue."

I gave her a smile. "Okay." I patted the blanket over her shin. "Well, I'm glad you're okay. And next Monday, if you're up for it, we can do surfing lesson attempt number two. Now that I know I'm getting lessons from the best."

"Oh, shut up." She pulled the blanket up a bit. "And tell K to bring me a brownie."

"Bernice! You're in here because of your sugar levels."

"Half a brownie then."

I rolled my eyes. "I'll pass the message on to K. But if he chooses to bring one or not, that's up to him."

She glared daggers at me. "Tell him to come see me." Then her tone softened, as did the look in her eyes. "Can you go get him for me, please. I have something I need to tell him."

Dane pulled on my arm. "Sure thing."

"We'll come and see you tomorrow, okay?" I said.

She smiled sadly and nodded. "I'd like that. Despite you being a pain in my arse."

I laughed and waved goodbye, and we found K sitting outside the main entrance. He looked calmer, even a little resigned, but he stood when he saw us.

"She wants to see you before we leave," I told him. "We'll wait right here." And you could see it, the flicker of hope in his eyes before he raced back inside.

"They'd be really cute together," Dane said, "if she'd give him a chance."

"It's kind of sad, isn't it? I mean, I'm pretty sure he'd move heaven and earth to make her happy, but she doesn't think she's worthy."

"It is sad," he agreed, "that she might have wasted all those years by not telling him the truth."

Something solidified in Dane's eyes and he was about to say something else, but people walked past and he looked at them instead.

I pulled him over to an unoccupied bench seat. "What's up?"

He squeezed my hand. "I really like what you told Bernice in there. It was sweet."

"It was true."

He nodded. "Yes, it was." He looked down at our joined hands and his eyebrows knitted together. "Griffin, I—"

"There you are," K said, interrupting us. He was smiling from ear to ear. "Dunno what you said to her, but she wants to talk... about everything when I get back."

I stood up and grinned at him. "That's great! And I didn't really say much at all. Her hang-ups have nothing to do with you, you know that right? It's not that she thinks you're not good enough. It's about her. She thinks she's not good enough."

"Oh, son. I've known that for as long as you've been alive."

Dane stood up and clapped K's arm. "Then we better get you home so you can hurry and get back here."

K beamed, his grey hair and wiry beard catching the sun like steel wool. "Yeah. God forbid, I keep her waiting fifty years or anything."

I laughed at that, and we walked to my car. Dane drove again, and when we'd gone a few blocks, I turned and looked back at K. "Is she really Bunny Warren?"

K gave me a knowing smile. "I could tell you some wild stories about her, but she'd kill me."

"She's told me a few stories of her travels and that she could surf and skate, but I never clued in that she was famous." The corner of my mouth pulled down. "To be honest, the name only kind of rings a bell with me. I'll have to google her when I get home."

"Don't believe everything you read on the internet," K

said, then he sighed. "She is the one and only Bernice Warren, nicknamed Bunny because of the rabbit warren thing. She hated it at first, but then she found it gave her some separation from the fame. She could be Bernice on paper and no one knew who that was." He looked out the window for a moment, obviously remembering something. "We met in 1979, and we've been inseparable since."

"And you've been in love with her since then," I concluded.

"Since that very first day. She was this tiny thing with long blonde hair, carrying a board twice as big as her, and she was giving some guy from Argentina a lecture on wave etiquette. I think he cut her off a wave at Bondi, and by God, she was giving it to him." He sighed again. "I'd never seen anything more beautiful in all my life."

I smiled at Dane and he grinned right back at me. "Did you travel with her?" I asked K.

He nodded. "All over. I wasn't as good as her. Not many of us blokes were. She was better than most of us combined, but the world wasn't what it is today. The generation she was born into robbed her of world titles." He shook his head and his smile became rueful. "Didn't stop her from speaking up though. She pushed the boundaries and challenged the officials to get a start on the pro-circuit. There was nothing written back then to say women couldn't surf..."

I grinned at that. "So she hasn't changed, then?"

"She hasn't changed at all," K said. "Even after the skin cancer... She had the surgery and had to have some treatments, and she lost her hair... She was still beautiful. But the nerve damage to her arm was irreparable." He shrugged. "She lost some spark after that."

"She called herself a cripple," I admitted.

He shook his head fiercely. "She's anything but that."

"That's what I told her," I said.

He sighed again and stared out the window for a bit. "She's so bloody stubborn."

"Oh, and she wants you to bring in a brownie," I added.

He rolled his eyes but it gave way to a chuckle. "So bloody stubborn. If diabetes thinks for one second it'll stop her, it's got another thing coming."

We dropped him back at his car at the beach car park and drove back to my place. K pretty much followed us into the drive.

"Tell her we said hello," I said.

"Will do." He gave us a salute and hurried in through the front door.

Dane and I went round the back and trudged up the stairs and found Wicket sound asleep on his spot on the sofa. He greeted us sleepily, happily, and we let him out to pee, and just as we were about to close the door and shut the world out, K called out to us and took the stairs two at a time. "Here. I'm not taking her a full one, she can have half. You guys can have the other half." He handed over the brownie and was gone with a wave.

I closed the door and put the half-brownie on the kitchen counter. "Um..."

Dane shrugged. "We could order pizza, have that, and watch the kids' cartoon channel."

I laughed. "I guess we could." Then I grinned at him. "Or we could each have half now and crash on the sofa." I broke it in half and handed him his. Then I planted my arse on the couch and grinned at him.

He watched me for a second, then joined me on the sofa. "Wait, before you eat that, there's something I need to tell you."

CHAPTER SIXTEEN

DANE

"WHAT IS IT?" Griffin asked. He put his half of the brownie back on the coffee table. "You've been kinda quiet since the hospital. You okay?"

"Yeah, yeah, I'm fine." I blew out a breath. "It's just that I've been thinking. A lot. And today kinda brought it home, ya know?"

He took my hand but chuckled. "Um, no, not really. You want to tell me something?"

I took a deep breath and started again. "I don't want to be like Bernice and K."

"What? Old potheads?" He laughed. "Or finally taking a chance at happiness?"

"Yes, no, both." I shook my head. "I don't want to wait fifty years because it never felt like the right time, or because I think you're not ready to hear it, or I'll scare you off..."

"Dane," he murmured.

But right then, Wicket jumped up onto the coffee table, snatched up the brownie in his mouth, and hightailed it off again.

"Wicket, no!" I lunged after him, but it was too late. He'd eaten it.

Griffin stood beside me. "Will it hurt him?"

I whipped out my phone and quickly searched up if hash brownies were bad for dogs. "Um, I can't really find... some say yes, some say no. There's YouTube videos... What kind of idiot would tape themselves getting their dogs stoned?"

When I looked up, Griffin had Wicket under one arm and was getting his leash. "Come on. We're going. I'll drive. You call the emergency vet and tell them we're on our way."

He was already out the door, so I grabbed my keys and raced after them.

Thirty minutes later, while one vet took Wicket, Griffin and I sat there getting our arses chewed out by another.

We explained the brownie wasn't ours. We explained we would never do anything to deliberately harm him. We explained all that, but still, she was right to be pissed. It could have been fatal. Not just the hash, but chocolate wasn't good for dogs either.

The first vet came to tell us that Wicket would be fine and they were just running another test or two, before both vets left us alone in the waiting room, and Griffin sighed. "What a day."

It had been one helluva day. First surfing, then Bernice passing out on the beach and being in hospital, now Wicket at the vets...

Griffin leaned in and whispered, "If someone had told me I'd be getting my arse reamed this afternoon, I would have assumed it would have been you."

I burst out laughing just as the second vet came back in. "It's not funny," she said.

"No, we weren't laughing about the brownie. He just made a joke," I explained lamely.

She handed me the bill. I read the bottom amount. Jesus. "It's not funny at all."

She finally cracked a smile. "No. Next time, keep your edibles out of reach of the kids, okay?"

"They weren't our drugs," Griffin mumbled. But they kind of were, in the end; K had given it to us. But Griffin looked genuinely hurt by her words. "We love him" he said softly. "Dane's a real good dad and I'm... well, I'm like a dad to him too, kind of. Well, I want to be. And we wouldn't hurt him. In fact, he's so spoiled, it's not even funny."

I put my arm around his waist. "It's okay," I told him. "She said he's gonna be fine."

I think she realised then that we were together, not just two young guys who were irresponsible with drugs.

"I put it on the coffee table and I shouldn't have. It was stupid."

I kissed his temple. "He's fine," I reassured him.

The first vet appeared again, this time holding Wicket. A smiling, eyes half-closed, stoned Wicket.

I snorted and Griffin almost laughed. "Is he...?"

"Baked?" the vet asked. "Yes. It was only a small dose, but so is he. He'll be fine. It will run its course and he should be back to normal by morning. Don't leave him unattended tonight though. He might feel safer in a box, not somewhere he can hurt himself if he falls, okay?"

We both nodded and she handed him over. I took him and Wicket thumped his tail lazily, still grinning. Still stoned.

Griffin gave him a cuddle but he laughed. "This isn't funny. But, oh my God, his face." Then he rubbed my arm. "Let's get him home."

Griffin decided in the car that Wicket might feel better, safer, in his own home, and I had to agree, so we went back to my place. I laid Wicket in his bed and he zonked straight out, but I stood there and watched him for a little while. Griffin stood behind me and put his arms around my waist and kissed the back of my neck. "Is he snoring?"

I chuckled. "Yep."

"I'm really sorry I put it on the coffee table. I should have told K no or just thrown it in the bin."

I turned in his arms and wound my arms around his back. "It wasn't your fault. You didn't feed it to him. He stole it."

"But still…"

I leaned up and kissed him softly. "I love you, Griffin."

His eyes shot to mine. He blinked, then he slow-smiled. "Really?"

I nodded. "Yes, really. It's what I wanted to tell you earlier. Before Wicket ate the brownie. It's what I've wanted to tell you for ages, which is crazy because we haven't really known each other for that long, but I reckon I knew from the second you sent me that selfie of you and Wicket. I looked at that photo and I knew this man would change my life. And my mum said she knew she'd marry my dad the day she met him, and K said today that he loved Bernice the second he saw her, so it might be crazy, but it doesn't mean it's not real—"

He took my face in his hands and kissed me. Soft and sweet, but deep and tender, until we were both breathless. He rested his forehead on mine and met my gaze. "I love you too. It's not crazy. God, it's perfect."

I laughed and kissed him again. "And I think Wicket would love to have you as his other daddy."

He laughed and traced his fingers down the side of my

face, taking in every detail. "Finding him that day was the best thing that ever happened to me. Because then I found you."

"Finders keepers?"

"For always."

CHAPTER SEVENTEEN

Dane

SO I HAD this great plan. Well, it was great in my head, and everyone else thought it was pretty amazing, but what Griffin would think of it, I had no idea.

Okay, so maybe I had a pretty good idea that he'd say yes. Otherwise I wouldn't be asking. But taking on a new puppy was a huge responsibility, and if we were partners in life, it was probably something which I should consult with him about first. But then it wouldn't be a surprise, and I wanted it to be a huge surprise. I wanted to watch his face when he first saw the gorgeous brown eyes and her soft, floppy ears. She was a tiny little mixed breed, white and brown, with the softest fur I'd ever felt, and her long lashes owned me from the second I saw her...

God, this could all go horribly wrong.

He'd moved into my place not long after Bernice had put her house on the market. She got out of hospital and agreed to finally give in to K's affections and she moved in with him. Griffin moved in with me. We still kept in touch with Bernice and K—this whole grand plan of mine had actually been Bernice's idea first. It was her suggestion in a 'wouldn't it be funny?' way that planted a seed of the idea in my head.

And I hadn't planned on doing it so soon, but a quick search of the local animal shelters later, and I found the perfect little girl to join our family. I arranged a pre-forever-home meet with Wicket to make sure they were compatible, and of course they were. And then I had to wait a week while she had her final vet checks and immunisations, which gave me a few days to plan.

And oh God, this could all go horribly wrong.

"You know it won't," my mother said. And Bernice and K said. And Griffin's parents said. And his sister. And my brother. And Li. And God, had I asked everyone?

Yes, Dane. Yes, you did.

I told myself to breathe. This would all work out. *Stop being so damn nervous.*

I put the box under the park bench, then ran across the car park, opened the door, and slid onto the back seat of Bernice and K's car. We'd parked away from the bench, waiting, watching, keeping a very close eye on the box.

"You told him two o'clock?" Bernice asked.

It was five to two. "Yes," I replied, my stomach in knots. "I think I'm going to be sick."

"No, you won't," K said. "It'll be fine."

I tried to breathe.

"You told him to meet you where he first found Wicket?" Bernice asked.

"Yes!"

K took Bernice's hand across the centre console. "He'll be here. God, you two are as bad as each other."

Bernice let out a shaky breath. "I just want to know if he got the right message."

The right message. Yes, I'd sent him a text telling him to go to the car park at the national park and that I'd meet him there. He had the day off and so had I, but I'd told him I only had the afternoon off and that I'd meet him here. We could go for an anniversary hike. He could bring Wicket with him and it'd be like an anniversary tradition because we'd gone hiking on our last anniversary too.

God, even my thoughts were rambling.

Then his car pulled into the car park, close to the bench. A second later, his door opened and Wicket jumped out and Griffin followed.

Oh God.

Wicket ran off and sniffed around the grass and Griffin stretched, then fixed his shoelace. He looked around, he checked his phone, he gave Wicket a pat.

Jesus, Griffin, will you look at the box already!

Then thankfully Wicket sniffed his way over toward it. Griffin followed him but sat on the seat and didn't even notice the box.

"Bloody hell," Bernice whispered. "If it were a snake, it'd have bitten him."

My stomach twisted even tighter. At this rate I wasn't even going to be able to speak.

But then Wicket focused on the box. He pawed at it, then barked, and finally—*finally*—Griffin noticed it.

He slid it out from under the seat, then obviously thought twice about what could be in it. Okay, so maybe watching the movie *Seven* last week hadn't been such a good idea. He stood back from it like it could possibly have a severed head in it, but Wicket tried to nose his way into the top. Griffin pulled him back and held him in his arms well away from the box.

Then he heard it. The faintest little puppy-cry.

Griffin snapped his head around, then stared intently at the box.

"Get ready," K murmured.

Oh hell...

Holding Wicket with one arm, Griffin reached out timidly and lifted the flap of the box, then stood up straight and put his hand to his mouth. He put Wicket down and reached inside the box.

"Go, Dane," Bernice hissed. "Go now."

I got out of the car and started to run across the car park. I needed Griffin to be distracted, to not see where I ran from, and when I got close enough, I slowed to a walk.

Griffin was holding the tiny puppy like it was the most precious thing in the world. The look on his face took my breath away.

Or maybe that was from running. Or the nerves.

"What you got there?" I asked.

Griffin jerked his head up, and he smiled when he saw it was me. He was too preoccupied to realise my car wasn't here. "Look at what I found!" He gently stroked her little head. "Who would just dump a puppy? What kind of monster would do that to something so small?"

Okay, God, the nerves were about to give me a stroke.

I stepped right in close and kissed him on the cheek, and for a moment, so I could catch my breath and gather my nerves, I patted the little puppy on the head too. She really was the cutest thing, and the pink collar was just too adorable.

"Oh," Griffin said. "She's got a name tag..."

My heart stopped beating. "What does it say?" I knew damn well what it said. I'd had it specially made. The name tag had 'Will you marry me?' engraved on it.

He read the tag. He blinked, and he read it again. Then he stared at me. I nodded, and when I went to one knee, he started to cry.

Well, shit. That's not the reaction I was expecting.

"If you don't want to, it's okay," I blurted out.

He held the little puppy to his chest and put his free hand to his mouth. He blubbered something I couldn't quite understand, but then, making my heart stop squeezing, he nodded.

"Yes?" I asked, fighting back my own tears. Stupid nerves and stupid everything.

"Yes, of course, yes," he cried.

I stood up and threw my arms around him, careful not to crush the little dog. "Thank you. You just made me the happiest man on the planet."

He kissed me, then smiling, he pulled back and whacked my arm. "You asked me on a puppy?"

I laughed. "I asked you on the name tag." But it reminded me about the dog. "Oh, and this is our new addition. She doesn't have a name yet, though. I thought I'd leave that up to you."

His eyes widened. "A proposal and a puppy?"

I laughed. "Yes!"

He started to cry again, though he was laughing and sobbing into the puppy all at the same time, so I put my arms around him and held them both. He cried and nodded. "A proposal and a puppy," he mumbled. "It's the best thing ever."

"I asked your parents and they said yes. And I asked

Wicket and he said you're the second-best dad ever," I joked.

He pulled back, his eyes red and his nose snotty. "You asked my parents?"

I nodded. "And Bernice and K are waiting in the car. They were my wingmen in case it didn't go as planned."

Griffin sobered. "I would never say no. I found you, remember?"

I nodded. "Well, you found Wicket."

"Same thing."

I snorted at that. "Kind of."

"You're a package deal."

"Now the four of us are."

His bottom lip trembled a little and he nodded again. He put his hand to my face and kissed me. "Finders Keepers, remember?"

"Always."

~ THE END

DISCLAIMER: No puppies were harmed in the writing of this book

ABOUT THE AUTHOR

N.R. Walker is an Australian author, who loves her genre of gay romance.
She loves writing and spends far too much time doing it but wouldn't have it any other way.

She is many things: a mother, a wife, a sister, a writer. She has pretty, pretty boys who live in her head, who don't let her sleep at night unless she gives them life with words.

She likes it when they do dirty, dirty things... but likes it even more when they fall in love.

She used to think having people in her head talking to her was weird, until one day she happened across other writers who told her it was normal.

She's been writing ever since...

———

Find N.R. Walker at
nrwalker.net
nrwalker@nrwalker.net

The Spencer Cohen Series, Book Two

The Spencer Cohen Series, Book Three

The Spencer Cohen Series, Yanni's Story

Blood & Milk

The Weight Of It All

A Very Henry Christmas (The Weight of It All 1.5)

Perfect Catch

Switched

Imago

Imagines

Red Dirt Heart Imago

On Davis Row

Finders Keepers

Galaxies and Oceans

Evolved

Private Charter

Nova Praetorian

TITLES IN AUDIO:

Cronin's Key

Cronin's Key II

Cronin's Key III

Red Dirt Heart

Red Dirt Heart 2

Red Dirt Heart 3

Red Dirt Heart 4

The Weight Of It All

Switched

Point of No Return

Breaking Point

Starting Point

Spencer Cohen Book One

Spencer Cohen Book Two

Spencer Cohen Book Three

Yanni's Story : Spencer Cohen Book Four

On Davis Row

Evolved

Free Reads:

Sixty Five Hours

Learning to Feel

His Grandfather's Watch (And The Story of Billy and Hale)

The Twelfth of Never (Blind Faith 3.5)

Twelve Days of Christmas (Sixty Five Hours Christmas)

Best of Both Worlds

Translated Titles:

Fiducia Cieca (Italian translation of Blind Faith)

Attraverso Questi Occhi (Italian translation of Through

These Eyes)

Preso alla Sprovvista (Italian translation of Blindside)

Il giorno del Mai (Italian translation of Blind Faith 3.5)

Cuore di Terra Rossa (Italian translation of Red Dirt Heart)

Cuore di Terra Rossa 2 (Italian translation of Red Dirt Heart 2)

Cuore di Terra Rossa 3 (Italian translation of Red Dirt Heart 3)

Natale di terra rossa (Terra rossa 3.5)

Cuore di Terra Rossa 4 (Italian translation of Red Dirt Heart 4)

Confiance Aveugle (French translation of Blind Faith)

*A travers ces yeux: Confiance Aveugle 2 (French translation of
Through These Eyes)*

Aveugle: Confiance Aveugle 3 (French translation of Blindside)

À Jamais (French translation of Blind Faith 3.5)

Cronin's Key (French translation)

Cronin's Key II (French translation)

*Au Coeur de Sutton Station (French translation of Red
Dirt Heart)*

Partir ou rester (French translation of Red Dirt Heart 2)

Faire Face (French translation of Red Dirt Heart 3)

Trouver sa place (French translation of Red Dirt Heart 4)

Rote Erde (German translation of Red Dirt Heart)

Rote Erde 2 (German translation of Red Dirt Heart 2)

www.ingramcontent.com/pod-product-compliance
Lightning Source LLC
Chambersburg PA
CBHW050522190726
48284CB00003B/907